for MAGGIE

with love.

Jane Langton

The
Mysterious Circus

THE HALL FAMILY CHRONICLES

The
Mysterious Circus

JANE LANGTON

The Hall Family
Chronicles

HarperCollins*Publishers*

Library of Congress Cataloging-in-Publication Data
Langton, Jane.
  The mysterious circus / Jane Langton.— 1st ed.
    p.   cm. — (The Hall family chronicles ; 7)
  Summary: With the help of a mysterious stranger and the magical
gift he brought them from India, the Halls foil a new enemy's plan to
build a Henry Thoreau theme park across from their home.
  ISBN 0-06-009486-9 — ISBN 0-06-009487-7 (lib. bdg.)
  [1. Magic—Fiction. 2. Elephants—Fiction. 3. Circus—Fiction.
4. Cousins—Fiction. 5. Family life—Massachusetts—Fiction.
6. Concord (Mass.)—Fiction. 7. Massachusetts—Fiction.] I. Title.
II. Series.
PZ7.L2717My 2005   2004021506
[Fic]—dc22   CIP
                                                         AC

Typography by Larissa Lawrynenko
1 2 3 4 5 6 7 8 9 10

First Edition

For Norman and Ruth Hapgood

Contents

If you have built castles in the air,
your work need not be lost;
that is where they should be.
Now put the foundations under them.

—HENRY THOREAU
(from "Conclusion," the last chapter of Thoreau's Walden)

I

A FAINT TRUMPETING

WHAT IF YOU WERE a peg on a pegboard, bouncing around from hole to hole? And what if all your friends and relations were pegs too?

The pegs for the Hall family are all the usual colors—red, green, yellow, orange and blue—and they move in a small circle on the pegboard for Concord, Massachusetts.

But there's another peg made of gold. To include the golden peg, the board has to stretch far across the Atlantic Ocean and the continent of Europe and part of Asia, all the way to the Indian city of Bangalore, because this peg belongs to Prince Krishna.

But it's wrong to call him a prince, because there are

no princes in India anymore. To Eleanor and Eddy and Georgie he's just plain Uncle Krishna, because he's married to Uncle Freddy's sister Lily. Of course he was born in a royal palace. But the palace is now a school. Krishna and Lily moved out long ago, leaving most of their jewels behind and every one of their gold chairs.

But Uncle Krishna brought one thing with him from the palace, and it's a royal treasure, all right, a chest full of strange and interesting things. Most of them are gone by now, the diamond and the flag and the rubber ball and—what else had there been in the chest? Oh, yes, a set of tiny wheels and gears, but they are gone now too.

One by one Uncle Krishna had given them to Eleanor, Edward and Georgie, his nieces and nephew in Concord. The diamond had been a complicated puzzle, and the flag had led them far away—far away in space, that is. The wheels and gears had led them far away in time. And the little blue ball had been the most fantastic gift of all, because it stood for something huge and very precious.

Was anything left? Krishna unlocked the cupboard, took out the chest and shook it gently. Yes, something was still rattling back and forth inside.

He opened the chest and took out the treasure. As he put it in his pocket, there was a faint sound of trumpeting, like animals in a jungle far away.

2

Matilda Oozes In

O<small>N THE PEGBOARD</small> for the Hall family at No. 40 Walden Street there are five important pegs, as well as a few that don't really count. The important pegs belong to:

Uncle Freddy,
Aunt Alex,
Eleanor,
Eddy and
Georgie.

The pegs that don't count are for a lot of cats, but never mind them, and a flock of chickens, but never mind them either, except for the rooster. And of course on the faraway edge of the pegboard is the important golden peg for:

Uncle Krishna.

And of course there's another one for his wife:

Aunt Lily.

But we mustn't forget two other pegs smack in the middle of the board, pegs that don't move at all. One is for a piece of statuary in the front hall, a chipped plaster bust of the man who built himself a house at Walden Pond a long time ago and wrote a book:

Henry Thoreau.

The other motionless peg belongs to another statue in the front hall, the light fixture on the newel post, a bronze lady known as:

Mrs. Truth.

So far, so good. If these were the only pegs on the board, the game would be fun. But unfortunately there's another one. For years this horrible peg has been circling around the others, plotting and planning and trying to take over.

But now something amazing has happened. The enemy peg is gone, so you'd think everything would be perfect from now on. But the game isn't happening that way. No sooner did the old peg leave the board than a new one slammed down in its place—or rather, it *oozed* down.

And the new enemy is far worse than the old one because she is so sweet.

4

3

KICK THEM OUT!

ATILDA MACINTOSH WAS there at the bedside of her second cousin as he lay dying in Emerson Hospital. She wanted to hear his last words, because last words are often so inspiring.

To her surprise, his last words were peevish. "Kick them out," croaked the dying man.

"What did you say, Cousin Ralph? Kick them out? Kick *who* out?"

Ralph Preek reared up in the hospital bed, coughing and spluttering. His eyes bulged, and his hands clawed at the blanket.

"I almost did it," he croaked. "I almost threw them out on the street."

"Threw who out on the street, Cousin Ralph?"

Now her dying cousin's voice was an angry rattle, but he clutched at Matilda's arm and gasped, "The trouble is, they found a paper."

"A paper?"

"A document." Cousin Ralph groaned and fell back on the pillow.

Matilda leaned over him and whispered, "What kind of document was it, Cousin Ralph?"

Once again he pulled himself up, and then hundreds of last words began tumbling out of his mouth, the whole bitter story. "I had a vision, you see, Matilda. I mean, I could see it all so clearly. The whole mixed-up family would be thrown out. I could see them scuttling away down Walden Street, their books and papers tumbling out of wheelbarrows—yes, yes, I could see it all!—their shabby furniture bouncing on the grass, their pots and pans clattering down the porch steps, their plaster busts shattering on the sidewalk, that tin lady of theirs smashing to pieces on the street, and all those yowling cats kicked into the bushes. Oh, yes, I could see it all."

Cousin Ralph closed his eyes and fell back in a swoon. "What a shame!" he whispered faintly. "Too bad!"

"But who are they?" murmured Matilda, leaning still

closer. "Who is it, Cousin Ralph, that you want me to kick out?"

Her second cousin's face turned purple. "Their name is Hall. A bunch of troublemakers. Now that you're on the board of selectmen, you must find a way to kick them out."

"Oh, yes, Cousin Ralph," said Matilda, beaming. "I'm so proud to have been elected to the board, even though I'm so new in town." Then she frowned. "But dear me, I think one of the other people on the board is named Hall. Could Mr. Frederick Hall be one of the people you want me to kick out?"

At this Cousin Ralph's teeth chattered with rage, and he flopped back on the pillow. But then he gathered a last ounce of strength and crooked a trembling finger at Matilda. "Wait," he croaked. "I have another vision."

As Matilda put her ear close to his lips to hear his last hoarse whisper, a nurse peered in the door and ran for the doctor. By the time the doctor came hurrying in, it was too late, because the poor old chap had expired—but not before Matilda MacIntosh had understood his dying vision.

"Good-bye, Cousin Ralph," murmured Matilda. Then she snatched up her coat and hurried out of the hospital, because she was late for an important meeting of the selectmen, *and one of the selectmen was the bitter enemy of her beloved second cousin!*

As she drove out of the parking lot, Matilda promised Cousin Ralph that his last inspiring words would never be forgotten. They would be a sacred trust. In the person of Matilda MacIntosh they would live on in glory.

4

THEY'RE COMING!

*T*HERE IS ANOTHER WAY of looking at this story. Perhaps it's not only a pegboard with family pegs and a gold peg and a brand-new enemy peg; maybe it's more like a brook running through a field.

The Mill Brook was just an ordinary little stream, flowing under arching brambles, passing through a pipe under Main Street, and coming out again into the sunshine to make its way to the Concord River. But after the selectmen's meeting on the afternoon of the day Matilda's cousin died, it was no longer ordinary.

It had become a watery line dividing Concord citizens on one side from Concord citizens on the other.

*   *   *

Uncle Freddy came back from the meeting chuckling. As he pushed open the screen door, Aunt Alex came running out of the kitchen to answer the phone. He laughed as she snatched it up and said hello. "There's a new woman on the board," said Uncle Fred, pulling off his jacket. "And you'll never believe what she wants us to do."

But Aunt Alex was listening to the voice on the telephone. With shining eyes she handed it to him, murmuring, "It's Krishna."

"Krishna? Calling from India?" Uncle Fred whistled and took the phone. When he hung up a moment later, he shouted the news, "They're coming. Krishna and Lily are coming."

Aunt Alex clapped her hands and made a vow to clean the house from top to bottom. The rooster in the backyard crowed, and Eleanor, Eddy and Georgie ran into the front hall from the kitchen. They were thrilled. "Maybe he'll bring us a present," said Eddy.

"A gift from the mysterious East," said Eleanor.

"Like an elephant," said Georgie.

Eleanor laughed. "Oh, Georgie, Uncle Krishna can't bring an elephant, not all the way from India."

Uncle Fred laughed too. "Who cares about presents? Stop being selfish. It's wonderful that they're coming, with or without elephants."

"Right you are," said Eddy, grinning, and he galloped for the stairs, tweaking the plaster nose of Henry Thoreau and giving a friendly slap to the bronze lady on the newel post.

"Of course, of course," said Eleanor, and she ran upstairs after Eddy to look in the mirror and comb her hair. (Eleanor spent a lot of time these days combing her hair.)

Georgie lingered behind, thinking stubbornly, *maybe he WILL bring an elephant.* She remembered an old picture of elephants in India, a whole parade of elephants with maharajahs sitting on their backs. Uncle Krishna had been a prince. Maybe he still kept an elephant for a pet.

Only then did Uncle Fred remember what he had started to tell Aunt Alex.

"You know that new woman on the board of selectmen? You'll never guess what she wants us to do. How we laughed!"

"What does she want?" said Aunt Alex, her smile fading.

"You won't believe it." Uncle Fred guffawed and slapped his knee. "She wants us to vote for a Henry Thoreau Theme Park. And guess where she wants to put it?"

Aunt Alex looked worried and said she couldn't guess.

"Right here across Walden Street in the Mill Brook meadow. Isn't that ridiculous?"

"Well, I guess so," said Aunt Alex, but her face turned pale. "Georgie, dear, where are you going?"

But Georgie was out the door and hurrying down the porch steps and opening the gate and dodging across Walden Street into the trees beside the stream. She wanted to sit beside the Mill Brook and watch the water flow over the leafy bottom on its quiet way to the river.

5

They're Not Coming!

*B*UT THEY WEREN'T coming after all.

Uncle Krishna called again from Bangalore. There had been a flood. A great river had over-flowed its banks. He had to stay and help.

"But don't worry," he said. "I'm going to *wheeee-squeeee.*"

"What, what?" said Uncle Fred. Pushing closer to the telephone table, he stepped on a cat, and it yowled, drowning out the faint words from twelve thousand miles away. "Say that again?"

But it was no better this time. Two more cats joined the chorus, and the telephone kept squawking *bzzzzzz—squeeee.*

Uncle Fred shouted, "Well, of course we're disappointed."

Krishna answered, and for a moment his voice was loud and clear. "And we too are disappointed. But *wheeee-squeeee*—sending a substitute."

"A substitute? Oh, Krishna, we don't want a substitute, we want you and Lily."

"I think you will like Amanda *squeeee-bzzzzz*, but *bzzzzz-squeeee* a problem child, I'm afraid."

"A problem child? Who? Amanda?"

The cats were still yowling, and the telephone connection between Asia and North America was worse than ever. "*Whizzzz-squeeee* cares about is *squeeee-squeeee* squerkus.*"

"Squerkus? Squerkus?"

"Forgive me, Fred, I'm afraid I cannot—" Again Krishna's voice faded, and then it came back loud and strong. ". . . have to say good-bye."

"No, no, Krishna, don't say good-bye! Wait, tell me! What do you mean by *squerkus*?"

Krishna seemed to be answering the question, but then a mosquito took over the phone and the conversation between New England and India was over. Uncle Fred shook his head and walked into the kitchen to tell the sad news.

There were groans of dismay. "Oh, I'm so sorry," said Aunt Alex.

14

"No presents then," moaned Eleanor.

"Alas, no," said Eddy.

"No elephant?" whispered Georgie.

"No," said Eddy, grinning at Georgie. "No elephant, alas."

"But he said something else," said Uncle Fred. "He's sending a substitute, somebody named Amanda."

"Amanda?" said Eleanor.

"Who's Amanda?" said Eddy.

"I haven't the faintest idea," said Uncle Fred, "Do you think she might be American? Amanda doesn't sound like an Indian name. Anyway the poor girl seems to be a problem child. And then he said something like *squerkus*. What's a squerkus?"

Nobody had any idea except Georgie. She spoke up brightly. "A circus?"

But that was ridiculous. Aunt Alex rushed off to put on an apron, vowing to turn the house inside out. Oh, how she would clean! Aunt Alex was a teacher and a writer like Uncle Freddy, but now she was determined to dust and scrub and make everything absolutely perfect for Amanda, the visitor from India. She would start in the front hall. There were cobwebs on the ceiling and dust everywhere. Aunt Alex threw open the coat closet and dragged out the vacuum cleaner.

It was true that the room was a little grubby. But it was also true that it was no ordinary front hall.

Of course the radiator looked ordinary, and so did the umbrella stand and the worn carpet and the patched velvet curtains in the schoolroom doorway. But some very strange things had happened in this room. Aunt Alex had seen them happening.

The front hall of No. 40 Walden Street was like the cave of a magician.

6

The Magician's Cave

*S*ELECTWOMAN MATILDA MacIntosh lost no time in pushing forward her idea for a Henry Thoreau Theme Park in the Mill Brook meadow, right across the street from No. 40 Walden Street. She was already in touch with Dizzy Enterprises, the big company that was famous for making theme parks all over the world.

Matilda did not ask herself what the real Henry Thoreau might have thought about becoming a theme park. Who cared? Henry had been dead for more than a hundred years.

But things were different at No. 40 Walden, where Henry was a hero.

His plaster bust was part of the family. It stood quietly in the curve of the stairs, gazing in the direction of Walden Pond, where the real Henry had built his small house with his own hands and written his famous book.

And the other statue in the front hall was important too, the tall bronze woman on the newel post. She wore a funny banner on her dress like the ladies of the Grange. Her banner said TRUTH, but you couldn't call anybody that, so she was *Mrs. Truth* instead.

As a piece of furniture, she was not only elegant but useful. Her left arm was handy as a coatrack, and her right arm held a star-shaped lamp. When the lamp was plugged in, shafts of brightness shone on the radiator, the kitchen door and the doormat, and darting rays pierced the holes in the velvet curtain to splash spots and moons on the schoolroom wall.

There were no old books of magic spells in this magician's cave, nor any secret panel hiding the door to a sorcerer's grotto. And yet there was a kind of magical connection between the bronze woman on the staircase and Henry's plaster bust, as if the wire that ran down her arm from her star-shaped lamp were plugged into the white knob of Henry's head instead of the baseboard.

What if they talked to each other in the middle of the night? What if Henry opened his plaster mouth and whispered, *"Old shoes will serve a hero"*?

And then Mrs. Truth might say, *"What's that, Henry?"*

"I mean, you don't have to wear fine clothes to do fine things."

"Oh, Henry, how true! I do so agree."

And then Henry might say, *"Guess what? The true harvest of my life is a piece of the rainbow."*

"Now wait a sec, Henry, what's that about the rainbow?"

"I mean, the best things in life are around us all the time."

"Why, Henry, how true! How perfectly true!"

7

HE HATED THEM

"YOU MUST GO INSTEAD," said Krishna.

His nephew looked alarmed. "You mean to America?"

"Of course. To the house of my beloved brother-in-law Frederick Hall and his dear wife in Concord, Massachusetts."

"And the other three?" said his nephew sullenly. "They live there too?"

"Yes, of course. Eleanor, Edward and little Georgie—how you will love them!"

But that was the whole trouble. Krishna's nephew did not love them. He hated them. He was sick and tired of hearing about those delightful children in Concord,

Massachusetts, the two girls and the boy who were so charming and clever. And he knew exactly what his aunt and uncle were thinking—*Why couldn't Uncle Krishna's nephew in India be more like Aunt Lily's nephew and nieces in America?*

Krishna watched his young nephew slouch off to his room. Was the boy too young and foolish to be sent on this errand? Of course it was true that he had the family gift. In fact he had inherited it so powerfully that his uncle was afraid for him.

His extraordinary powers had been clear since childhood. Like other children, the boy had found playthings in the out-of-doors, but unlike the others, he could do astonishing things with his sticks and stones. When he climbed a tree, it burst into flower. When he picked up a shell, it rang with music. When he waded in a stream, it sprang up in fountains.

Could he be trusted in America to keep his power in check? Would he be a good guest? The boy was such a problem child! Always running away from school to see some traveling fair, or reeling up and down the road on that strange one-wheeled contraption he called a unicycle, when he should be doing his schoolwork.

But of course he must go. The boy must be an ambassador from Krishna and Lily to their Concord family, he must bring the new present to Fred and his wife and the darling children.

The new little gift would bring India to them, the real India, the best of India, the very soul of India. Krishna took the treasure out of his pocket, shook it gently, listened, and smiled.

8

A Handful of Stones

WHEN HE HANDED THE little gift to his nephew, Krishna warned him, "Be most careful with it. And bring nothing else—no musical shells, no amulets or rings."

"Uncle," said his nephew, "I have no amulets or rings."

"Well, good. Then you will bring only this."

"But my unicycle, uncle. I cannot go without that."

His uncle was shocked. "Your unicycle! But it's far too big for your suitcase." Then Uncle Krishna relented. "Well, I suppose we could pack it in a box. But nothing else, boy, do you hear me?"

So in the end Krishna's young ambassador set off for

the airport with nothing but his backpack, his unicycle and, in one of his pants pockets, the tiny present for the American family.

Nothing else? Well, hardly anything else. His other pocket sagged with a handful of stones.

At the airport terminal in Bangalore Uncle Krishna shook his hand and smiled. "Do you have your plane ticket? Your money? Your passport?" And then he drove away, calling a last command from the car window, "Give everyone my love."

Love? Krishna's nephew had no love to give. But when his uncle's car was out of sight, he laughed with delight. He was free. From now on there would be no kindly uncle failing to see the dreams inside his head, no dear aunt gazing at him in loving bewilderment, no stern schoolmaster asking impossible questions, no guidance counselor shaking her head in despair. He was alone. He could do whatever he wanted.

Therefore why should he bother with a long droning flight to Boston in a jet plane, and then find his way from the airport to the town of Concord?

In fact, why should he talk to those hateful people at all? He would ride his unicycle right up to the horrible house at No. 40 Walden Street, knock on the door, hand over the present, and then—why not?—he would speed away and make all his dreams come true.

There was a little green park across the road from the terminal. Krishna's nephew knelt on the sidewalk beside the great glass revolving door, unpacked his unicycle, and wheeled it across the street into the park, rattling the stones in his pocket.

9

MATILDA'S SACRED TRUST

AROOM-VAROOM. The vacuum made so much noise, Aunt Alex didn't hear the knock at the door.

Only when a shadow fell across the floor did she look up and see someone peering through the glass. At once she turned off the vacuum, but Georgie was already there, opening the door.

A woman stood outside, smiling at Aunt Alex and Georgie. "Oh, how do you do," she said. "My name is Matilda MacIntosh." She grasped Aunt Alex's hand and gave it a hearty shake. "Oh, I've heard so much about you! I'm so glad to meet you at last!"

Georgie shrank back into the shadows, but Aunt

Alex was charmed. How did this smiling woman know anything about her? "Won't you come in?" she said, swinging the door wide.

At once a couple of cats streaked past the visitor's legs. Matilda hated cats, and she squealed and skipped sideways. Then she tittered and said, "Oh, no. I haven't time now. I just want to ask a question. Tell me, is that field across the street the Mill Brook meadow?"

"Why, yes, it is," said Aunt Alex, "because the Mill Brook runs through it. You see, a long time ago it was dammed up to make a pond, and there was a mill there, but then—"

"Oh, thank you, thank you!" Laughing joyfully, Matilda hugged Aunt Alex and whispered in her ear, "I've heard such wonderful things about you. I want us to be the best of friends."

"Why, certainly," said Aunt Alex. Confused and flattered, she watched the woman hurry away down Walden Street, look back and wave.

But later on, when Aunt Alex went outdoors to weed her flowerbed, she saw her new friend across the street. Matilda MacIntosh was walking in long strides among the trees beside the little stream and scribbling in a notebook. It was almost as if she were measuring the distance from tree to tree. But no, surely she was only a nature lover, studying the wildflowers.

27

A butterfly fluttered up from a daisy in Aunt Alex's weedy garden, and she smiled, because she too was a nature lover. It would be something to have in common with her new friend. As she turned to go indoors, a little breeze ruffled her hair. Was it true that the flapping of a butterfly's wings in China could start a wind that grew into a storm at sea?

Well, no, of course it wasn't true. It was just a saying. *Big things have small beginnings*—that was all it meant.

Across the street Matilda MacIntosh was carrying out her sacred trust, her promise to her dying cousin Ralph. She scribbled a last note—

Width of meadow 500 ft.

—and clapped her notebook shut.

10

THE PRINCESS IN THE TOWER

ON THE DAY THE mysterious stranger came wobbling up Walden Street on a unicycle, Eleanor sat in front of the mirror in her bedroom and saw that she was gorgeous. She had seen it coming, and now it was a fact.

No longer was she a tall, skinny freckled kid with wispy red hair, and arms and legs like sticks. She had plumped out, she had frizzed her hair and she was as glamorous as anybody else in her high school class. It felt wonderful to be glamorous. Eleanor ran downstairs to show herself to everybody.

There was a pounding from below. Eleanor clumped down the basement stairs and found her brother hammering nails. "Hey Eddy," she said, "what are you doing to that piece of wood?"

"Making stilts." Eddy wrenched out a bent nail with the claw of the hammer.

"Well, good for you," said Eleanor. Then she plucked at his sleeve. "Stop for a sec, Eddy. Look at me."

Eddy stopped and looked up. "Your shirt's buttoned wrong," he said calmly, and went back to hammering.

Eleanor stumped back upstairs and found Uncle Fred in the schoolroom. "Look at me, Uncle Freddy," she said, leaning across the desk, planting her elbows on his book.

But he only smiled and said, "Are you ill, Eleanor dear?"

"Oh, Uncle Freddy." Eleanor laughed and went looking for Georgie, because Uncle Fred was really hopeless. His mind was high up over the roof with the Oversoul, which was a cloud of beautiful thoughts floating around over Concord.

Georgie was upstairs in her bedroom with her friend Frieda. They were lying flat on the floor with their heads bowed over a long piece of shelf paper.

"What are you kids doing?" said Eleanor.

"It's Noah's Ark," said Georgie, looking up with shining eyes.

"All the animals in the world," said Frieda importantly.

Eleanor bent down to look. There were certainly a lot of animals on the paper—giraffes and hippos, bears and wolves, lions and tigers. Georgie had made a long parade of elephants with her colored pencils. "Well, good for you," said Eleanor, giving up and hurrying away downstairs. Funny little Georgie! She was too busy to notice that her big sister had become as pretty as a movie star.

Behind her, Georgie and Frieda began to argue. "What about dinosaurs?" said Frieda, sitting up and sucking her pencil. She had drawn all the animals she could think of.

"But they're extinct," said Georgie.

"I know they are," said Frieda, "but it would be fun to draw them just the same."

"Oh, yes, it would," whispered Georgie.

"Dibs on Tyrannosaurus rex," said Frieda, flopping down again.

Downstairs in the kitchen Eleanor found Aunt Alex. She was standing on a stool with her head in a cupboard, scrubbing the shelves for Amanda. "Oh, please, Aunt Alex, won't you look at me?" said Eleanor.

Aunt Alex took her head out of the cupboard. She said nothing, but she stepped down from the stool, took off her rubber gloves, patted Eleanor's cheek, and murmured, "My pretty girl."

Eleanor was glad. The others might be blind, but not Aunt Alex. Satisfied, Eleanor went back upstairs, threw open the window of her room and leaned her elbows on the sill to show herself to the world.

The curtains streamed out and so did Eleanor's long hair. She felt like Sleeping Beauty or Snow White or some other famous princess in a fairy tale.

It was at that very moment that a mysterious young man on a unicycle came wheeling along Walden Street, swooping in circles and juggling at the same time. Keeping his eyes on his little silver balls as they flew high over his head, the stranger caught sight of Eleanor, the storybook princess, looking down from her tower.

Surely she was one of his hated cousins? Staggered, Krishna's nephew teetered wildly on his unicycle, lost his balance, and tipped over with a crash.

II

THE MYSTERIOUS STRANGER

WHEN ELEANOR SCREAMED, they all ran out of the house and stood around the fallen stranger—that is, all of them but Eleanor, who was still craning her neck out the window, staring down at the boy who lay crumpled on the street with his silver balls bouncing all over the road.

Aunt Alex knelt beside him and felt his arms and legs. Then she stood up and said, "I don't think anything's broken." The stranger's eyes were closed, but he rolled over, groaning.

"Hey, look at the traffic," said Eddy, because a truck was waiting, revving its engine and honking its horn, *blat blat.*

"I'll handle it," said Frieda briskly. At once she took a commanding position in the middle of Walden Street, whistled through her teeth and held up her hand.

"Don't be so dumb," said Eddy. "They've already stopped."

But Frieda was barking an order. "Georgie, you take the other side."

"Me?" said Georgie. "Well, okay." Turning around, she held up a timid hand.

"Come on," said Uncle Fred, "let's carry him inside." Eddy lifted the stranger by the shoulders, Uncle Fred took him by the ankles, and together they carried him to the side of the road. Aunt Alex picked up the unicycle, Frieda gave a mighty wave to tell the cars and trucks to move on, and Georgie scrambled after the stranger's scattered silver balls.

One of the drivers leaned out and yelled at Uncle Fred, "You want I should call the police?"

"No, thank you," said Uncle Fred. "Open the gate, please, Georgie."

Another car pulled up and a woman called out, "You ought to take that boy to the emergency room."

The boy's eyes opened. "No, no," he said feebly.

Aunt Alex called to the woman in the car, "He'll be all right."

The woman looked cross. As she drove away she

34

shouted back at them, "Don't forget, I'm a witness. I saw the whole thing."

"What does she mean, she's a witness?" said Eddy, as they laid the stranger down on the sofa in the hall.

Wincing, he lifted his head. "She means I can sue you, and then she will say it was your fault." Then the stranger dropped his head back and moaned. The left side of his face was puffing out and turning purple.

"Quick, you two," said Aunt Alex to Georgie and Frieda, "I need a bowl of water and a towel." Then Uncle Fred leaned over the wounded boy and asked him where he lived.

There was a pause, as if the stranger were choosing between Alaska and New Jersey and Paris, France. "I come from India," he murmured at last, closing his eyes again.

"India!" said Eddy. "Hey, wow, do you know our uncle Krishna? He used to be the prince of Bangalore."

The stranger lay still, but the brown skin of his left cheek turned pink. "Why, yes," he said slowly. "I think I have heard of him."

"Well, then, maybe you know Amanda too?" said Eddy. "There's this girl named Amanda. She's supposed to be coming."

"Amanda!" The stranger opened his eyes again, and turned his head to look at all five of them. The dignified man in the sweater must be Uncle Krishna's old friend Frederick Hall. The tall woman must be Mrs. Hall. One of the little females must be that dumb girl Georgie, and of course the boy who was looking at him so eagerly, waiting for an answer, was his hateful cousin Edward. Where was the one called Eleanor, the female cousin who had stared at him out the window?

She chose this moment to make her grand entrance as the fairy-tale princess in person, floating downstairs in a gauzy shawl. But the shawl was too long. Eleanor tripped, missed the bottom step and fell flat. Her long skirt slid up to her knees, showing her big sneakers.

The stranger sat up with a jerk, while Aunt Alex rushed to help Eleanor stumble to her feet. Snickering, Eddy said, "Allow me to introduce my ugly sister."

12

THE PRESENT

*I*T WAS THE RIGHT HOUSE. This was the fabled family he had been looking for, the family he had hated from half a world away. Krishna's nephew sat up, glowering, but he was feeling better.

"Are you staying around here somewhere?" said Uncle Freddy. "Where were you going just now?"

"I was looking for—please, one moment." The stranger had a formal way of talking. He pulled a scrap of paper from the torn pocket of his shirt, and said, "Is this not Number Forty Walden Street?"

Uncle Fred laughed. Eleanor threw her shawl over the arm of Mrs. Truth and laughed too. They all laughed. So did Frieda, but then she said good-bye and hurried away. "I'll tell everybody," she said importantly, slamming the screen door.

Aunt Alex smiled at the stranger and said, "Well, you've found us." She handed him a pill and a glass of water. "This will help your poor head."

"But my dear boy," said Uncle Fred, "why did you want to come here in the first place?"

"And hey, what's your name anyway?" said Eddy.

There was another pause. Once again the stranger seemed to be choosing among possible answers—John? Theodore? Robert? Then he said shyly, "Andy. Just call me Andy."

"Andy!" Eddy was surprised, because it didn't sound like an Indian name, although the boy looked very much like a visitor from that part of the world, with his dark skin and shining black hair.

Uncle Fred tried to put two and two together. The boy came from India and he was looking for No. 40 Walden Street. Had he come from Krishna? Was he the problem child? The one who cared about nothing but—whatever it was—*the squerkus*? But no, he couldn't be that one, because Krishna was sending a girl, not a boy. A girl named Amanda.

Aunt Alex had a roll of gauze. Wrapping it around the stranger's head, she asked him where he was staying.

Uncle Krishna's nephew thought it over. It was true that he was free now, as free as air, and therefore he could live anywhere. But for the moment what should he do? Perhaps they would let him stay right here. Of course he hated every one of these people, but he wouldn't have to stay with them very long, only until he found the perfect place for his heart's desire.

Looking up at the man in the old sweater, he waved his arms helplessly, as though he had no idea where he might possibly stay.

"Well, why don't you stay here?" said Eleanor boldly, glancing sideways at Aunt Alex.

Georgie clapped her hands, Uncle Freddy smiled, and Eddy said, "Hey, cool."

"Why, of course he can stay here," said Aunt Alex, heading for the stairs. "I'll just run up and change the sheets in the back bedroom."

But the boy called Andy stood up shakily and said, "Wait."

Aunt Alex turned back and stared at him in surprise, because suddenly he seemed so different. Even with a bandaged head and a purple cheek he looked almost majestic. He was feeling in his pants pocket. "I must give you something in exchange."

"Oh, no," said Uncle Fred. "You don't need to do that."

39

"A present," said Andy. "I want to give you a present from India." He looked around at the five of them, wondering which one to give it to. The smaller girl wasn't as hateful-looking as the others. "Here, little one," he said, "hold out your hand."

The present didn't look like much. It was only a big seed, shiny and red, with a white thing growing out of one side. Andy shook it and it rattled. Then he handed it to Georgie and said, "Be very careful with it."

"Oh, yes, I will," breathed Georgie reverently, closing her fist around it gently. "I promise."

13

THE FIZZING BRAIN OF
MATILDA MACINTOSH

*A*T THE NEXT MEETING of the board of selectmen, to Uncle Fred's horror, another member declared herself in favor of the theme park in the Mill Brook meadow—Annabelle Broom.

Annabelle was now Matilda MacIntosh's best friend. She was thrilled by the way Matilda kept knocking on her door and hugging her and whispering, "I've heard such wonderful things about you."

It had taken Matilda only two visits to Annabelle's house to close the deal. The two of them sat huddled together at Annabelle's kitchen table while Matilda opened her heart and unfolded her deepest feelings. Annabelle had feelings like that too, and she confessed them to her wonderful new friend. So of course when it came to a vote, she sided with Matilda about the theme park.

"It's horrible," cried Uncle Fred, running into the house and slamming the door. "The vote is now two to three. That terrible woman needs only one more vote to take that stupid theme park to Town Meeting."

Aunt Alex was scrubbing the kitchen floor. (There was still no word from the girl called Amanda, but when she came at last, she would find everything clean as a whistle.) "Fred dear, back up." Dabbing her mop around his feet, Aunt Alex said comfortingly, "Surely nobody else on the board will vote for it."

But Aunt Alex did not know Matilda MacIntosh. She did not even know that her new best friend was a member of the board of selectmen, the one Fred was always raging about—*that terrible new woman on the board*. Nor did Aunt Alex understand the creative power of Matilda MacIntosh's brain.

It never slept. Matilda was simply bursting with ideas about her Henry Thoreau Theme Park. Just think what a blessing it would be for the town of Concord! People would come from all over the world because Henry Thoreau was an international celebrity!

Furthermore, since his shack at Walden Pond was gone, why couldn't they build a nice new one for him in the theme park? And why couldn't they dig a mini–Walden Pond in the meadow and put his new house right beside it?

And that wasn't all. One morning Matilda woke up with another idea, and she bounced out of bed to scribble it down. *Henry would be there in person.* What a glorious idea! It was truly wonderful what people could do these days with robots. They could make one out of fiberglass with a lot of machinery inside so that Henry could roll out of his house on little wheels and open his mouth and speak. He could say something or other from his book. That book of his was just chock-full of stuff that he could say. They could install a loudspeaker in his head and connect recorded messages to buttons on his shirt. *Digital! It would all be digital!*

Matilda's brain was really fizzing. Her head reeled as she thought of the money her theme park would make for the town of Concord. But of course, she reminded herself severely, the profit wasn't the important thing. The really terrific selling point would be something else entirely.

The Henry Thoreau Theme Park would be *educational*, that was it. So educational for all the little children!

14

THE JUGGLER

S O THE BOY CALLED Andy moved into the back bedroom with his juggling balls and his unicycle.

Aunt Alex asked no questions. She shortened some of Eddy's clothes and laid them on Andy's bed. Eddy didn't mind sharing his T-shirts and pants. He was pleased to have this interesting new friend, right here in the same house.

Eleanor was pleased too. She had lost interest in being a fairy-tale princess because it was too much work, and besides it was really dumb, but she liked having Andy in the house as a friend—although it was strange that he didn't act very much like a friend himself.

Georgie was pleased too. Every night she hid the red seed under her pillow, and every morning she tucked it deep in her pants pocket. The seed had a stopper, but Georgie didn't pull it out. She had promised to take good care of Andy's present, and she would keep her promise. She had taken care of precious things before. She knew how to be careful.

As for Andy himself, after living for two weeks at No. 40 Walden Street, he was still trying to get used to his new name. He had come to the right address, and he had done what Uncle Krishna had told him to do. Was it time to go home?

The trouble with going home was that his uncle would still forbid him to do the one thing he wanted to do more than anything else in the world. Instead he would be sent back to school.

Andy hated school. Here in Concord, school was over. What if he stayed all summer with these people? It was true that he hated them—well, most of them. He had begun to think better of Aunt Alex, and there was nothing to hate about little Georgie.

But Georgie's Uncle Fred was too much like Uncle Krishna—always talking about that foolish Oversoul and about somebody called Henry. As for Eleanor and Edward, they seemed friendly enough, but Andy suspected they didn't really like him at all.

Never mind. He was here and he was free. Why not follow his heart's desire right here in this little village, so far away from home? There was nobody here to tell him not to.

So Andy spent his days exploring the town of Concord on his unicycle. Whirling up and down Walden Street and Main Street and Sudbury Road, he kept looking left and right, hoping to find the right place.

Today he would look again. But now it was time for breakfast. Although Mrs. Hall's pancakes were sometimes a little burned, they were delicious. Andy had three helpings with butter and maple syrup.

Edward had three helpings too. Mopping up the syrup on his plate with his last forkful, he said, "Hey, Andy, I want to show you something down cellar."

"Well, all right." Doubtfully Andy followed his cousin Edward down the cellar stairs.

"See?" said Eddy, proudly displaying his new stilts.

"But they are so short," objected Andy. "I have seen a man on stilts ten feet high."

Eddy's were only one foot high. "Well, give me a little time," he said crossly. "I'm just getting started."

Andy's shrug was a little scornful. Silently he went back upstairs to his room, opened his backpack and took out his juggling balls, because he had thought of a sensational new trick. First he practiced his old tricks with six of the silver balls. Up they went, one after another, and fell lightly back into his hands. He juggled them behind his back and under his knees, never dropping a single one.

But the ceiling was too low for real juggling. Andy opened the window and leaned out to look around. He saw nothing but the chicken yard, the laundry line and a butterfly on a honeysuckle bush. The air was quiet. The shirts on the line hung still.

So there was no one to see him, only the chickens and the butterfly. As Andy tossed up his first ball, the butterfly fluttered up and the shirts began to lift and fall back.

The light wind breathed on Andy's face, but it was not too strong for juggling. He tossed up a second ball, a third, a fourth, a fifth, a sixth.

Ah, that was better. Here under the open sky there was no ceiling. Up went his silver balls, higher and higher, as high as the roof, as high as the chimney, as high as the top of the pine tree. At last Andy tossed one ball highest of all, and watched it fly up and up, becoming smaller and smaller until it merged with the blue sky.

The others fell back into his hands. Smiling, he closed the window.

He had not noticed Aunt Alex, because she had been feeding her chickens behind the hen house, scattering

47

cracked corn all over their little yard.

But Aunt Alex had seen Andy. She had seen him juggle his balls as high as the roof, as high as the chimney, as high as the pine tree. And then she had seen one of his silver balls fly straight up into the sky and disappear.

Where had it gone? What did it mean?

Bewildered, Aunt Alex thought about it gravely as she watched her little rooster jerk his head up and down and snatch at kernels of corn. But then she remembered about tomorrow, and she hurried indoors to bustle around the kitchen.

What should she make for tomorrow? Gingerbread? A cake? Matilda MacIntosh was coming to tea tomorrow—*for a cozy chat*, she had said, *with her darling new friend.*

15

THE SCUFFLE

*E*DDY CARRIED HIS STILTS outdoors and stalked around the front yard, *clomp, clomp,* with his big sneakers a foot above the grass. When Andy came out with his unicycle, Eddy pranced around, trying to show off. It was a mistake, because he lost his balance, staggered forward, floundered backward, and had to jump off. Sheepishly he said, "Whoops."

Andy said nothing. *How could his cousin be so clumsy? His stilts were so short!* Then Andy mounted his little bike and wobbled toward the sidewalk. Eddy called after him, "Hey, Andy, where are you heading this time?"

Careening into the road, Andy shrugged again—*It's*

none of your business where I'm going—and reeled down Walden Street, heading south.

Eddy watched him go. What was that grumpy kid doing, anyway? He kept wandering off on his unicycle, disappearing for hours at a time. And why was he so stuck-up? Disgruntled, Eddy dumped his stilts on the porch and went inside.

In the front hall he found Georgie and Eleanor sitting side by side on the sofa. Georgie was unrolling her long piece of shelf paper to show Eleanor the animals of Noah's Ark—her elephants and jungle animals and Frieda's Tyrannosaurus rex.

Eddy felt peevish. "Hey, look," he said, badgering Georgie, "stop being such a wimp. What's the use of having that little red thing Andy gave you—some present!—if you don't look inside?"

Georgie stood up and said, "I don't want to look inside." Stubbornly she put her hand in her pocket and closed it over the red seed.

"Attagirl, Georgie," said Eleanor, jumping up too. "Stick to your guns."

"Look inside what?" shouted Oliver Winslow, barging in the door. Oliver was an old friend of Eddy's. He was a big gawky kid with huge muscles and a goofy grin.

"Oh, Georgie's got this little thing in her pocket," said Eddy. "It's got something inside but she won't let us look."

"No kidding," said Oliver. Snickering, he grabbed Georgie's arm and pulled her hand out of her pocket. "Come on, Georgie, give us a look."

"Oh, Oliver, stop it," shouted Eleanor. "Let her alone."

"Oliver, you big jerk," yelled Eddy, but he was laughing.

Georgie held fast, but Oliver pulled back her fingers, snatched up the seed and held it high over his head, crowing joyfully, "Looky here what I've got."

In despair, Georgie pulled at his shirt. "No, no, oh, please, Oliver, please give it back."

Eleanor and Eddy tugged at his arm. "Oliver, you big dumbhead," shouted Eddy. "Oliver, you pig," screeched Eleanor.

But Oliver was enjoying himself. Grinning, he tramped around the front hall, dragging them after him, Eddy shouting, Eleanor screaming, and Georgie wailing, "Please, oh, please."

It was a wild four-sided scuffle. In the confusion the red seed slipped from Oliver's clumsy fingers and dropped to the floor. It bounced twice, the stopper fell out and the contents lay scattered on the floor.

"Oh," gasped Georgie, because they were elephants, tiny carved elephants. Dropping to her knees, she scooped them up in her hand, counting, "One, two, three, four, five, six, seven—"

The others got down on the floor too and tried to help. It wasn't easy, because the little carved elephants seemed to be wriggling all over the floor.

"Eight, nine," said Eleanor, snatching at two more.

"Ten," said Eddy.

"Eleven," said Oliver, feeling a little ashamed of himself.

Carefully Georgie poured the elephants back in the red seed, and tried to push in the stopper. It was a struggle because the little elephants were hooting faintly and trying to tumble out. Patiently she nudged them back inside and fastened the stopper tight.

Then she stood up slowly and pocketed the red seed without a word.

Eleanor, Eddy and Oliver stood up too, and Oliver said, "Hey, Georgie, I'm sorry." But then he reared back in surprise, because something was swelling up out of the floor.

They had to back away, because it was pushing at their legs, thrusting them up against the wall.

They had missed one of the elephants.

16

THE GRAY BALLOON

*I*T WAS LIKE A BALLOON, a gray balloon, swelling and swelling, puffing out enormously in all directions.

The balloon shoved Eleanor and Georgie against one wall and Eddy and Oliver against the other. Eleanor squealed and put her arm around Georgie and backed into the coat closet.

"Don't worry," shouted Oliver, as Eddy disappeared behind a bulge. "It's just a balloon." He jerked a penknife out of his pocket, pulled out the blade and tried to jam it into the swelling rubber side.

But it wouldn't go in. The balloon did not burst with a pop and begin to shrivel. It was not made of rubber. It was hard and solid and wrinkled and leathery. Four huge legs were expanding beneath it, and suddenly a colossal head blooped out at one end, sporting a long gray trunk.

The balloon was an elephant, a real live elephant. Lifting its trunk to the ceiling, the elephant bellowed and swayed and stamped a gigantic foot.

The house had not been built for elephants. The timbers shook, the windows rattled. Aunt Alex's desk collapsed and the lamp crashed down. Pictures smashed on the floor. In the schoolroom the books tumbled from the shelves. In the kitchen the teacups swayed on their hooks and the hanging pots bonked and clashed. Upstairs the cats squealed and scrambled under beds. Dressers slid sideways.

Pressed against the wall by the massive haunch of the elephant, Eddy punched it with his fists, shrieking, "Stop."

Oliver butted it with his head, bawling, "Stop it, you dumb elephant."

But the elephant did not stop. It kept right on swelling, bulking larger and larger in the narrow front hall, growing more and more enormous.

Eleanor and Georgie were safe in the coat closet, but Eddy and Oliver had to squirm sideways, squashing their faces against the elephant's belly. Inching crabwise to the door of the schoolroom, they fell backward

54

through the velvet curtain. At once they sat up, gasping for breath, and pulled the curtain aside. Horrified, they watched the stair railing bend and break, rammed by the elephant's ballooning side. The banister burst and the spindles snapped and Mrs. Truth toppled from the newel post, drooping at a dangerous angle. Her star-shaped lamp trembled and the connecting wire tore apart in a shower of sparks. And something even worse was happening.

Peering between the elephant's four giant legs, Eddy saw the plaster bust of Henry begin to totter and fall. "Catch him!" he shouted. "Oh, quick, somebody catch him."

And Aunt Alex was there, just in time. Rushing in the front door, she dropped her bag of groceries, lunged forward and caught Henry's heavy head only inches from the floor.

Then all at once everything settled down. The elephant stopped trumpeting. It stopped growing bigger and bigger. Its back nudged the ceiling, but that was all. Instead of bursting through to the second floor and shattering the bedroom ceilings and bringing down the roof and destroying the house entirely, the elephant merely lowered its trunk, flapped its ears gently and craned its neck to look mildly around. By good luck there was just enough room for its great domed head in the space

55

where the stairs turned left at the landing.

The house stopped shaking, the pots stopped clattering, the teacups hung still, the jittery cats crept out of hiding, Mrs. Truth held fast at an angle of forty-five degrees, and everything quieted down.

Eddy and Oliver crawled between the mighty front and back legs of the elephant. Eleanor and Georgie crept out of the coat closet and bumped after them on hands and knees. Then all of them scrambled to their feet beside the wrecked staircase where Aunt Alex stood frozen, clutching Henry's plaster bust.

Together they stared up at the colossal animal that was packed so tightly inside the walls of No. 40 Walden Street, crowding out every trace of the shabby nobility of the front hall.

The very air was pushed aside, the dusty familiar air with its faint taste of enchantment. There was no longer any room for enchantment in their own front hall.

No room for enchantment? What about the elephant? If the elephant wasn't enchantment, what was?

17

WHAT NOW?

WHEN ANDY'S UNICYCLE swirled back up the street, he was alarmed by the way the house seemed to bulge outward. As he leaped from his bike, a piece of the porch railing sagged and fell into the bushes.

He galloped up the steps, looked through the screen door, and saw nothing but a gray wall. The wall had a tail. It was the back of an elephant.

An elephant! That little girl had broken her promise! He shouldn't have trusted her!

Andy darted down the porch steps, raced around the house, threw open the back door and stared up at the massive head. At once the elephant reached out its trunk and curled it around Andy in a gentle hug.

Whispering words in one of its big ears, he stroked the wrinkled trunk, and then untangled himself. Had this great creature trampled the good people who had welcomed him so kindly? Oh, yes, how kind they had all been, every single one of them! Andy's anger fell away. He had been wrong about them from the beginning.

Dropping to his knees, he looked under the elephant's belly. At once he saw two pairs of legs—Eleanor's and Georgie's. "Are you all right?" shouted Andy.

At once Eleanor stooped and he could see her looking at him upside down. "Come on, Georgie," said Eleanor, and together they thumped toward the back door on hands and knees.

Andy reached out, gripped Georgie by the shoulders and pulled her out on the back porch. Eleanor crawled from under the elephant by herself. Dodging its swaying trunk, she stood up shakily beside Georgie.

The three of them looked at one another with pale faces. Nobody said anything. The crisis was too horrible, the elephant too big.

But then there was a shout from Eddy and a holler from Oliver. They had run up the front stairs and started down the back. They were halfway down.

Squeezing past the elephant's left ear, they tumbled out the door.

Andy slammed the screen door shut, and Eleanor grasped Eddy by the arm and hissed at him, "Aunt Alex, I don't see Aunt Alex."

"Oh, she's okay," said Eddy, breathing hard. He put his face against the screen and shouted, "Hey, Aunt Alex."

At once she called from upstairs, "I'll be down in a minute."

Aunt Alex had taken charge. Stumbling upstairs with Henry's head in her arms, she had figured out the whole crazy thing:

1. It was incredible that there should be an elephant in the house.
2. But there WAS an elephant in the house.
3. The elephant was facing the back door.
4. The elephant was too big for the back door.
5. Therefore the back door would have to be made bigger.
6. They would have to call a carpenter.

Aunt Alex dropped Henry's heavy head on her bed and called Mr. LaRue.

18

TIM-*BERRR!*

*H*E CAME AT ONCE.

Mr. LaRue was an old friend of the rickety house at No. 40 Walden Street. Over the years he had shored up sagging floors, patched the roof, jacked up the porch, replaced the diamond in the attic window with a piece of glass and done a lot of other things to keep the old house from falling down.

He didn't seem surprised to find an elephant in the front hall. He said, "Tsk, tsk," and pulled a wrecking bar out of his toolbox. For the rest of the morning, under Mr. LaRue's direction, they took apart the rear wall of the house.

Luckily the back stairs went all the way down to the

basement, so Eddy was able to squeeze past the elephant again—this time it patted his back with its trunk—and hurry downstairs and return with his arms full of tools. At once he attacked the porch railing with a crowbar.

Oliver Winslow snatched up a sledgehammer and gave one of the supporting posts a smashing blow. There was a splintering crash as it toppled and the roof slumped sideways. "Tim-*BERRR!*" roared Oliver.

"Hey, Oliver, watch it," shouted Eddy, ducking out of the way.

"Later," scolded Mr. LaRue, shaking his head. "Not now."

"Allow me to help," begged Andy. He picked up another crowbar and began prying loose the boards beside the back door. Andy was feeling guilty, even though the elephant in the house was not really his fault. Now, working side by side with Eddy, heaving with all his strength on the crowbar, he felt more and more ashamed of himself. His cousins were not hateful after all. In fact they were really quite *cool* (it was a word he had picked up from Eddy).

There were *skreeks* from the nails and groans from the loosened boards and crashes from the sledgehammers. Soon the entire porch railing collapsed into the ferns beside the back steps.

61

Eddy mopped his brow and grinned at Andy, and Oliver looked around joyfully for something else to smash. Before they could stop him, he had bent the garbage can and flattened a couple of lawn chairs. He was about to shatter one of the laundry poles when Aunt Alex screamed, "Stop," and snatched the shirts off the line.

"Come on, Georgie," said Eleanor, brandishing a handful of screwdrivers. "We'll work on the porch steps." Patiently they sat on the bottom step and wrenched at the screws. Before long the planks were free. Georgie and Eleanor picked them up one at a time and dropped them in a clattering pile beside the chicken yard, while the hens fluttered wildly up and down and the rooster had a fit.

Meanwhile, inside the house, the elephant stood waiting calmly, watching the wreckage with friendly interest and poking its trunk through the opening to feel the air.

At last Mr. LaRue stepped boldly over the doorsill, held up his tape measure against the elephant's side, reared his head back and stared up at the part he couldn't reach. "I estimate this elephant to be eight feet, nine inches high," he said importantly, snapping the tape measure shut. Then he jerked it out again to measure the new gap in the house wall. "Couple more inches," he said briskly, and got to work at once with a cross-cut saw.

By the time Uncle Freddy came home from the library and heard the shouting and ran around the house to gasp with horror at the disaster in the backyard, they had built a ramp of boards and Andy was urging the elephant outside.

"Come on, my good girl," he said, backing up in front of it, encouraging it to move out of the house and down the ramp. *"Phut-a-phut."*

The elephant eyed the ramp uneasily, moved one huge leg forward, then drew it back.

"Girl?" said Eddy. "It's a girl?"

"Of course she's a girl," said Andy. He reached out and stroked the elephant's trunk. "I am going to call her Sita. Come on, Sita, it is all right." He whispered something in the elephant's ear, and at last she stepped carefully onto the ramp. When she was halfway down, the boards cracked under her weight but she blundered ahead, and soon she was standing safely on the grass—immense and astonishing, but perfectly at home in the backyard, just another household pet like the cats and the chickens.

The chickens didn't think so. They scrambled around, squawking in terror, while the gallant little rooster peered up at the monster towering over the hen yard and crowed, *Stand back, surrender, kneel!*

But Eddy laughed with delight and reached up to pat Sita's fat side. Eleanor and Georgie stroked her trunk, and poor Uncle Freddy reeled with dismay. *His childhood home, wrecked by a passing elephant!*

Was it the fault of the boy from India? Or a trick by the mysterious missing Amanda? Or was it simply another dangerous gift from his old friend Krishna in Bangalore? As a present, what a mistake! What could they possibly do with an elephant?

But the elephant was leaving. Uncle Freddy watched, open-mouthed, as it bowed its great head before the boy who called himself Andy. At once the boy scrambled up on its back and sat down, draping one leg over the elephant's ear.

As Sita began lumbering down the driveway past Mr. LaRue's pickup truck, Andy looked back at Eddy and Eleanor and said, "Good-bye, you guys." (*You guys!* It was another comical American way of talking.)

"Good-bye?" cried Eleanor. "What do you mean, good-bye?"

"I will be back," called Andy, and then he was gone, rocking easily on Sita's back as she turned out of the driveway and shuffled down Walden Street, heading in the direction of his dream.

"Well, that's that," said Mr. LaRue, brushing sawdust off his pants.

He turned to Uncle Freddy. "You want I should build her up again?"

Uncle Freddy pulled himself together and croaked, "Well, of course."

"Lunch first," said Mr. LaRue. He climbed into the cab of his truck, ate a peanut butter sandwich and took a nap.

Poor Uncle Freddy shook his head, stumbled up the broken boards of the ramp and went inside, completely bewildered. Eddy and Eleanor followed him into the ruins of the front hall.

"I just don't understand," groaned Uncle Fred, surveying the wrecked staircase and the drooping statue of Mrs. Truth.

Aunt Alex had put away the laundry upstairs, and now she came down, careful not to brush against Mrs. Truth's half-fallen lantern. "Fred, dear," she said, and at once she started to tell him what had happened. Eddy waved his arms around and explained it at the same time. So did Eleanor. They were all talking at once. Still befuddled, Uncle Freddy lifted his hands in despair.

None of them noticed that Georgie had not followed them into the house. Georgie was hurrying along Walden Street behind Andy and the elephant, trying to keep up.

19

THE BOSSINESS OF MATILDA MACINTOSH

*G*EORGIE WAS NOT THE only one interested in the elephant. Cars were slowing down. The drivers didn't seem to mind being held up. They were thrilled to see a giant pachyderm shuffling calmly along Walden Street. Soon traffic was backed up in both directions.

One of the cars belonged to Matilda MacIntosh. Matilda was on her way to visit another darling friend and fellow selectwoman, Jemima Smith. Astonished by the elephant, she honked her horn, *beep-beep.*

Andy didn't care about the honking horn, but when he looked around and saw Georgie hurrying along behind him, he urged Sita onto the grass beside the road.

At once the drivers speeded up a little, still staring, watching Andy reach down and lift Georgie up beside him.

Matilda MacIntosh did not drive on. Instead she slowed down and parked her car smack in front of the elephant.

Matilda had inherited bossiness from her family. Bossiness went all the way back to the MacIntoshes of the Scottish highlands. And now that she was a Concord selectwoman, she could really throw her weight around.

To Matilda the elephant looked like trouble, and she had a nose for trouble. *Nip it in the bud,* Cousin Ralph always said. *Kill it before it multiplies.*

Now the elephant was again moving ponderously into the street. Matilda stepped out of her car and stood bravely in its way, holding up her hand.

At once the elephant reached out its trunk in kindly greeting, but Matilda jumped back in alarm.

Trembling, she looked up at the little girl on the elephant. Hadn't she seen the child before? And then, smiling sweetly at the boy, she said, "May I ask, young man, if you have a parade permit?"

The boy looked at her blankly for a minute, but then he smiled too.

He reached inside his shirt and—*presto*—pulled out a scroll of parchment.

Georgie watched Andy unroll the scroll, and then

she listened in amazement as he read the ancient script
aloud:

> *This document grants to the bearer the freedom of*
> *all avenues, streets, roads, superhighways and*
> *mountain passes under the stars.*

Georgie gasped. The scroll was signed by:

Adam and *Eve.*

20

A Message from Noah

MATILDA MACINTOSH FELL back in confusion. Sita plodded into the middle of Walden Street again with Georgie and Andy swaying comfortably on her back. But soon they came upon another obstacle, the fire and police station. A couple of police officers were working outside in the sunshine, washing a patrol car. As the elephant came in sight, they dropped their sponges and stared.

Andy gave them a friendly wave, and so did Georgie. But then a car whizzed up beside the patrol car and slammed on its brakes. It was Matilda MacIntosh again. Matilda had come to her senses. Leaping out of her car, she hurried up to the policemen and said eagerly, "Allow me to introduce myself. My name is Matilda MacIntosh.

As a member of the Concord Board of Selectmen, I am proud to meet the heroic men of the Concord Police Department! How do you do!"

The policemen gaped at her, gaped at the elephant, gaped again at Matilda.

"And now," she said firmly, "I must ask you to get this creature off the public highway. It is holding up traffic."

The two men turned their heads to look at Sita, because she was moving on again, edging around Matilda's car and gliding in her rolling shuffle along Walden Street, with her riders rocking from side to side on her back.

"Well, I'm jiggered," said the first police officer, whose name was Bill.

"If that don't beat all," said Barney, the second police officer.

Matilda couldn't believe it. She flapped her hands and cried, "But I insist. You've got to stop them. Can't you see? They are endangering public safety. You must demand to see their license."

"Their license for what?" said Bill, grinning at the elephant, because Sita was doing a clever trick right before his eyes. She was turning herself around in a circle and finishing with a sort of ponderous two-step.

Matilda saw it too. "Look at that!" she cried. "Do they have a license to perform animal acts on a public street?"

"Oh, well, what the heck," said Barney. He loped after Sita and called up to Andy, "Hey, listen, I guess you need a license to perform like that in public. That's what this lady says anyway."

Andy and Georgie looked down at him. Then Andy grinned, reached into his shirt and brought out another parchment scroll. This one looked as old and important as the first. Serenely Andy unrolled it and read it aloud:

This document grants to all the beasts of the earth the right to dance for joy.

(signed)
Noah

Smiling at Barney, Andy handed down the document. Barney looked at it and whistled. "You mean like Noah in the Bible?"

Bill read it too and shook his head in wonder. "You mean *that* Noah? Noah with the ark and all the animals?"

"And the rainbow?" said Barney. "You mean Noah with the rainbow?"

"But, but," sputtered Matilda, "you can't let them. I mean, it must be against the law."

But the police officers only laughed, and waved Sita forward. "If it's okay with Noah," said Bill, "it's okay with me."

21

THE CIRCUS TENT

ONLY A LITTLE WAY PAST the police station a broad field opened up on the other side of the road, just past the public garden plots with their cabbages and tomato plants and sunflowers, and beyond the public school. Andy had found it yesterday. It was the perfect place for his heart's desire. Now he urged Sita across Walden Street and into the field.

Georgie didn't care where they were going. Two years ago, when she was only in the fourth grade, she had walked boldly out of the house at No. 40 Walden Street, opened the gate, and marched away on a long journey—all the way to Washington to deliver a message to the president. Now on Sita's back she would gladly travel a thousand miles, ten thousand!

But this journey was a short one. The great elephant slowed her pace, and now Georgie could hear a wonderful noise. It was like the *oompah* of a marching band and the *rub-a-dub* of a drum, and her heart beat fast.

Andy's knees nudged Sita to a stop at a place where a great ring of white cloth lay on the grass. It was a tent, an enormous tent. To Georgie's surprise, it was not made of canvas. It was a ring of gossamer silk spread out in a broad circle on the weedy field like a filmy veil or a spider's web beaded with dewdrops.

On the grass within the ring lay two long poles like the masts of a sailing ship. In the very center of the ring between the poles, a crazy contraption was making a din, tootling and rattling and thumping with mechanical horns and whistles and whirring belts and drums. There was so much noise that Andy had to shout at Sita.

At once she bent her two front legs and knelt, and he slipped off her back to the ground. Then Sita reached up her trunk, wrapped it around Georgie and set her gently down.

Andy smiled. "Georgie," he said, "may I have another one?"

For a moment Georgie was puzzled, but then she understood. Quickly she reached into her pocket for the red seed. But then she hesitated and said, "Are you sure it's all right? The first time—I mean, I didn't want it to happen. I was keeping my promise, really and truly."

Andy laughed, and said, "You are a good little girl after all. Yes, it is all right now, really and truly."

At once she handed him the red seed from her pocket. Andy thanked her, and then he pulled at the stopper with delicate fingers and shook out one of the tiny elephants. Turning, he flung it high in the air. Together they watched it glide softly down and land on a tuft of grass.

Georgie had seen it before, but again she was awestruck as another gray shape surged up from the ground, right out here in the open, and swelled larger and larger and huger and huger, until another massive elephant stood towering above them, nodding its great knobbed head.

This one was far larger than Sita. At once it stretched out its immense grey trunk to touch Andy's shoulder as if to say hello, and then the enormous trunk moved sideways to brush Georgie's cheek.

She stood perfectly still, trembling with joy. It was as if a king were touching her with his sword to proclaim her a knight-errant: Sir Georgie!

For a wild moment she wished she had a handful of peanuts to offer in thanks, but at once she saw that it would be an insult. Peanuts for a king? Never, never.

Then Andy spoke up again, calling the elephant "Rajah," and Georgie knew she had been right, because a rajah was a king. Now he was pointing and giving directions. "*Phut-a-phut,*" he said again.

Rajah nodded his huge head and lumbered away. In spite of his enormous size, he stepped delicately across the grass. Then Andy murmured to Sita, and she followed Rajah.

While Georgie stood out of the way, Rajah wrapped his trunk around the end of one of the tent poles and lifted it a few feet off the ground. Then Sita wound her trunk around it to steady it, and Rajah set his massive head against it and shoved with all his enormous strength.

The pole rose and rose until it stood erect, carrying up with it the gauzy tent. The delicate fabric was tied to the pole with silvery cables and silken ribbons. Then Rajah and Sita pushed and pulled to lift the second pole.

Soon both poles stood steady and firm. Above them, between the two peaks of the tent, sunshine streamed through a round opening, throwing a ring of light on the ground.

And in the middle of the ring the music began again, the *oompah* and *rub-a-dub* of the calliope. It was only a mechanical band, but the tinny music was playful and carefree. Georgie clapped her hands as the belts whizzed around and the pipes wheezed and the cymbals clashed and the drumsticks rattled out the tune of "Yankee Doodle, Yankee Doodle, Yankee Doodle Dandy."

22

AT LAST!

OF COURSE IT WASN'T as big as the three-ring circus that came to Bangalore every year from France, nor the one from Mexico that traveled all over India with an enormous tent and a merry-go-round and a Ferris wheel and a carnival. But small as it was, it was a circus. It was Andy's own circus at last.

Uncle Krishna had not believed in the circus. "How foolish, dear nephew," he had said. "You must forget about the circus." And then he would go on and on about his favorite subject, that dusty old Oversoul of his. "You see?" he would say at last. "There are higher things to think about, dear boy."

Higher than the circus? Higher than the brave men

and women who flung themselves through the air at the top of the great tent? Higher than the brave walkers on stilts ten feet high? Higher than the pyramids of men and women standing on one another's shoulders? And how could anything be higher, really and truly, than the funny clowns? Or higher than the parades of mighty elephants? Nothing! Nothing could be higher! Nothing in the world!

And so he had always shrugged his shoulders and sulked, and then Uncle Krishna would shake his head, disappointed. He had never understood about the circus!

But now it was happening. It was all coming true, Andy's circus at last. With shouts and screeches, a throng of kids—little kids, middle-sized kids, and big kids—came running across the field.

23

FRIEDA ON THE PHONE

*F*RIEDA HAD ORGANIZED the whole thing. She had walked into Georgie's house, she had seen the wrecked staircase and the hole in the back wall, and she had shrieked at Oliver Winslow, "What *happened?*"

"Oh, it was just this elephant," said Oliver, shrugging his shoulders. "You know, really huge."

"An *elephant!*" Frieda looked around wildly. "Where's Georgie?"

Oliver shrugged again and said *he* didn't know where the little kid was, and Frieda ran upstairs, jumping recklessly over the drooping statue of Mrs. Truth.

Georgie was not in her room. Frieda clattered

78

downstairs again, shouting, "Well, where is she?"

But nobody knew where Georgie was.

"She was out in the backyard a little while ago," said Eleanor.

"Maybe she's in the attic," said Eddy, and he charged up the stairs. But when he came down, he was shaking his head.

"Oh, Frieda, dear," cried Aunt Alex, throwing down the broom—she had been sweeping up sawdust and bent nails—"I thought she must be at your house. Have you seen Georgie, Mr. LaRue?"

Mr. LaRue didn't know one child from another. He shook his head and licked his pencil and scribbled a list for his trip to Concord Lumber:

6 clear pine 1 x 4s, inside/outside casings
2 plywood 8 x 4s
8 cedar clapboards
10 yds. weather stripping
3 sheets drywall
1 roll joint tape
1 qt. vinyl compound

Looking over Mr. LaRue's shoulder, Uncle Fred wanted to ask how much all that stuff was going to cost. Instead he plunged down cellar to look for Georgie.

But then Oliver had the right answer. "I'll bet she went after that stupid elephant," he said, grinning at Frieda. "Crazy little kid."

"The elephant!" exclaimed Frieda. "Which way did it go?"

"Thataway," said Oliver, wagging his shaggy head and pointing.

"I'll go after her," cried Aunt Alex, flinging open the front door.

But Frieda said, "Wait a sec, let me handle it." She pulled her cell phone out of her pocket, held it in a grip of steel and jabbed Rachel Adzarian's number, because Rachel lived just down the road.

"I saw it," cried Rachel. "Just now, I saw the elephant. It was heading into the field beside my house, and Georgie was sitting on it. And so was this other guy I never saw before."

"Okay, Rachel," barked Frieda. "From now on your house is command headquarters. Call Sidney. Tell him to get there really fast. Call Hugo."

With a wan smile, Aunt Alex let Frieda take charge, remembering the way she had organized the great pilgrimage to Washington, keeping sixteen thousand kids marching in perfect order. The kids had come from all over the country to join Georgie's great children's crusade, flooding along the highway while Frieda shouted commands and kept everybody in line, that whole army of little kids.

Eleanor took Frieda's orders too. She got on the phone and called Otis Fisher. "Hey, you bet," said Otis.

She called Cissie Updike. "I'll bring Carrington," cried Cissie.

Eddy and Oliver didn't wait to call anybody. They threw open the door and took off for Rachel's headquarters right away.

So they were the first to arrive. But within fifteen minutes, thirty-four other kids were milling around Rachel's house. Mrs. Adzarian was astonished, but like a good sport she mixed up batches of frozen lemonade and tore open a package of potato chips.

The biggest kid under Frieda's command was Oliver Winslow. The smallest was Carrington Updike. Carrington had been only a baby in a stroller on the march to Washington, but now he could toddle around by himself.

The next smallest was Weezie Hoskins. Nobody had phoned Weezie because she was such a pain, but she had heard about it somehow, and she was there. She began by pinching Carrington, making him howl. At once Carrington's big sister Cissie slapped Weezie, who howled even louder.

"Okay, you guys," shouted Frieda, fumbling in her

pocket for her police whistle, "you gotta get in line."

"Where to?" bawled Oliver.

"I don't know exactly," cried Frieda, walking back-ward. "Just everybody get in line."

But then there was a glitch. Somebody shouted, "Stop!"

It was Matilda MacIntosh, leaping out of her car in Rachel's driveway. Matilda had rushed off to the Town Hall for an official paper, and now she was waving it.

"Permission," she cried. "You've got to have permis-sion to hold a public gathering."

"But that's silly," said Frieda. "This isn't a public gathering, it's just us kids."

Oliver grabbed the paper out of Matilda's hand and said joyfully, "Well, well, what have we here? Why, good gracious me, this won't do at all," and he tore up the paper and threw the pieces in the air. Carrington caught one with a happy scream and ate it. Matilda gasped.

"Okay, you guys," cried Frieda, lifting her arm high. "Onward!"

Her whistle shrieked, and at once they were off, run-ning across the field past the garden plots and dodging around the school toward something exciting. Above the trees they could see the white peaks of a tent, and now there was music, thrilling music, thumping and clashing and tweedling "Yankee Doodle."

Matilda got back in her car. *They're only kids,* she said to herself. *Surely I can handle a bunch of snotty little kids.*

But Matilda didn't know Andy. She didn't know Georgie. And she certainly did not know Major General Frieda (Napoleon Bonaparte) Caldwell.

24

WHO WANTS TO JOIN THE CIRCUS?

*T*HEY SWARMED OVER the circus ground like ants. They darted inside the tent to see the mechanical cymbals jerk up and down and the mechanical drumsticks batter the drum, and then they ran outside to yell hello to Georgie and admire the elephants. Georgie beamed at them, and Sita and Rajah stood massively in place, rocking gently from side to side and swaying their great trunks in greeting.

Frieda couldn't stand it. All discipline had disappeared. She blew her whistle and made everybody line up to be introduced to Andy. Of course Andy already knew Eddy and Eleanor, but he didn't know anybody else. "Andy, this is Sidney Bloom," said Frieda imperiously.

And then she introduced Rachel Adzarian, Otis Fisher, Cissie and Carrington Updike, Weezie Hoskins, Hugo Von Bismarck, Oliver Winslow and all the rest.

"Oh, and Hunky Poole," said Frieda in dismay. *What was Hunky doing here? Hunky Poole was even more of a pain than Weezie Hoskins.*

But Andy was delighted to meet everybody, even Weezie Hoskins and Hunky Poole. He shouted, "Who wants to join? Who wants to join the circus?"

There were screams of joy, "Me, me," and a forest of arms waggled in the air. Everybody wanted to join. They all wanted to do circus tricks with Andy in the gauzy tent that had appeared so suddenly in the open field between Walden and Thoreau Streets, right here in their own hometown.

But what tricks could they possibly do? Sidney opened his hands helplessly. "The trouble is," he said, "I don't know any circus tricks," and Rachel said, "Me neither."

"I will teach you," said Andy. "Who wishes to be the strong man?"

Well, that was easy. Oliver hollered, "Me."

"Who would like to ride bareback?"

"Me, me," cried Cissie Updike. "I mean," she said importantly, "because I take these riding lessons, so I already know how."

"Who wishes to be the grand marshal in a top hat?"

"Oh, I'll take care of that," said Frieda, because she had been a grand marshal all her life, ever since she had bossed her family around in baby talk.

Four days went by before Aunt Alex and Uncle Freddy really understood what was happening. They had been too busy working on the house.

They spent the first day helping Mr. LaRue board up the back wall with big sheets of plywood. On the second day they helped with the repair of the stair railing, holding the spindles upright while Mr. LaRue hammered them back in their holes. "Toenailing, that's what you call it," he mumbled through the nails in his teeth.

On the third day they helped him haul the statue of Mrs. Truth back up on her newel post. At last she was standing erect again, only a little skewed to one side. Her lamp was still dark, but Mr. LaRue said, "Tsk, tsk," and wired up a new connection.

But even without visiting the circus grounds, Aunt Alex and Uncle Fred heard about it every morning at breakfast, and also after breakfast when everybody took over the kitchen making lunch, with Georgie scraping the bottom of the peanut butter jar and Eddy poking around in the refrigerator and Eleanor showing Andy how to make tuna-fish sandwiches.

"Look, Andy," she said kindly, handing him the

mayonnaise, "just spread this stuff on the bread. There's nothing to it."

And then at the supper table they were full of it again. Eleanor and Eddy did most of the jabbering, while Georgie beamed and Andy just sat there glowing.

Some of their stories were a little alarming. Aunt Alex and Uncle Fred looked at each other with startled faces. Collapsing in bed after supper on the third day, Uncle Fred said, "Why don't we just walk over there tomorrow?"

"And see for ourselves," agreed Aunt Alex. "I'm sure they're all right, but—"

"Exactly," said Uncle Fred. "We'll just go over and take a look."

25

Matilda's Solemn Vows

*T*HE CIRCUS WAS NO SECRET. The families knew, and all the drivers on Walden and Thoreau Streets wondered what was happening, because they could see the white peaks of the tent above the treetops, right there in plain sight.

Matilda MacIntosh also knew what was happening. The circus was a plot by those people at No. 40 Walden Street, the very ones Cousin Ralph had warned her about with his dying breath.

And he was right. That man Fred Hall was a menace. His ranting and raving against the theme park was a pain in the neck. The other selectmen were so confused, they couldn't decide how to vote.

But Matilda was a determined woman. She had already promised Cousin Ralph to do her best to get rid of those people. Now she made two more solemn vows:

1. Come hell or high water, the board of selectmen WOULD vote for her theme park in the Mill Brook meadow, and so would Town Meeting.
2. The silly little circus WOULD BE TERMINATED.

It was as simple as that.

Matilda decided to make another visit to No. 40 Walden Street. Perhaps she could charm her darling new friend into putting the screws on her husband. After all, what was a wife for? If she, Matilda MacIntosh, had a husband, she would wind him around her little finger.

But when Matilda knocked on the Halls' front door, no one was at home because Aunt Alex and Uncle Fred were strolling down the street to the circus grounds.

Matilda gave up, hopped back in her car and whizzed around the corner to call on Annabelle Broom. Then perhaps she would pay a visit to Jemima Smith. Both Annabelle and Jemima were on the board of select-men, and they were both *such darling new friends*.

Walking into the tent, Aunt Alex and Uncle Fred admired the way the sunlight shone through the walls as if they were made of alabaster. And then they clapped their hands and shouted "*Bravo,*" because the elephant—the one who had wrecked their front hall—was lumbering toward them with Eleanor on her back, and Eleanor looked so pretty in her old dancing-class tutu.

She waved at them, laughing and pointing her toe. (Eddy's ugly sister had given up being a fairy princess, but her gorgeousness certainly came in handy in the circus.)

Then after the elephant came Eddy, stalking on his stilts. He was six feet off the ground! "Not high enough yet," he said, jumping down. "It's wicked easy."

Aunt Alex opened her mouth to warn him to be careful, but then Oliver Winslow shouted at them, "Hey, Miz Hall, Professor Hall, watch this."

It was the human pyramid. "Up you go," said Oliver, lifting Sidney Bloom over his head to sit on his shoulders. Then Cissie Updike clambered up to sit on Sidney's shoulders, and her little brother Carrington was handed up like a sofa pillow by Oliver and Sidney, and then Cissie reached down and lifted him on *her* shoulders. Carrington threw out his arms like a pro and crowed with delight.

90

Good heavens, Carrington Updike was only a baby. Aunt Alex started forward in alarm, but Uncle Fred held her back. "They'll be all right," he said, although he was a little scared himself.

The human pyramid collapsed neatly. Cissie dropped her little brother into Oliver's arms and scrambled down Sidney's back. Sidney jumped boldly down from Oliver's shoulders and landed with a thump. Then Oliver tossed Carrington in the air a few times, and Carrington chuckled with joy.

Cissie ran across the ring to brag to Georgie's family about her other job in the circus. "Hey, guess what? I'm going to ride my horse bareback."

"Well, good for you, Cissie," said Aunt Alex faintly, and then it was Otis Fisher's turn to show off his juggling act.

Otis wasn't very good yet. He kept dropping his Indian clubs. When one of them fell on his head, he winced, then picked it up and tossed it again, explaining, "I just need a little more practice."

26

A JOB FOR HUNKY POOLE

*T*HERE WAS A LOT MORE to do. Andy kept pulling important things out of nowhere.

"Hey," said Hugo Von Bismarck, "that top hat, where'd you get that?"

Andy looked at the hat in his hand as if puzzled. "I think it was behind a bush."

"It's for me, I think," said Frieda promptly. Taking the hat, she jammed it down over her ears.

Hugo was still baffled. "But what about all those poles and cables for Sidney's high-wire act? They weren't here yesterday."

Like all magicians from the beginning of time, whether their enchantments were real or only clever pretending, Andy kept to himself the spells in his head, the stones in his pocket, the strange transforming power that had come down in his family, the gift he shared with Uncle Krishna.

"I am sorry, all you guys," he said, shaking his head as if he couldn't remember. "I guess they must have been behind another bush."

"Oh, no," chuckled Hugo, "those things would never fit behind a bush."

"It was a big bush, I think," said Andy. "A really big bush."

"Oh, is that it? Hey, that's really cool." Hugo grinned with understanding. "I guess people dump stuff behind bushes all the time, right?"

And then there was the hay. The sweet-smelling mountain of hay bales was far too big to have turned up behind a bush. "What's all that hay doing here?" said Eleanor.

"It's for Maizie, silly," said Cissie, looking down from her horse, which was not a beautiful white stallion with a flowing mane but an old gray nag with a broad back.

"And for the elephants, I'll bet," said Georgie. She looked up at Andy with shining eyes. "May I take care of the elephants?"

But Andy said, "No, no, Georgie. There is something else I want you to do." He pointed to the top of the tent.

"Do you see it up there? Your trapeze?"

"A trapeze! For Georgie?" Eleanor was horrified. "But that's so dangerous!"

"No, it is not dangerous," said Andy. "It is perfectly safe. I will be with her. And anyway, if she were to fall, the net would catch her. But she will not fall."

"Well, I don't know," said Eleanor. "Aren't you scared, Georgie?"

But Georgie wasn't scared. She was thrilled, because she had flown before. She had flown high over Walden Pond, night after night, with the great bird she had called the Goose Prince. *It's really strange,* thought Georgie, *but Andy reminds me of him, just a little.*

There were too many kids and not enough jobs. Rachel Adzarian ran after Frieda and begged, "Oh, please, Frieda, what can I do?"

Frieda's top hat kept slipping down over her eyes. She pushed it up and looked solemnly at Rachel. "You're good at art, right, Rachel?"

"Well, sort of," giggled Rachel modestly.

"Well, then," said Frieda briskly, "we need a lot of flags. Can you make flags?"

"Well, I guess so. What kind of flags? American flags?"

"No, no. Red, orange, yellow, green, blue, purple. Lots and lots of flags. We'll put them up all over." She glanced at Andy. "Okay with you, Andy?"

"Of course," said Andy. "I mean, that is very cool." He grinned at Frieda. As grand marshal of the circus, she was perfect.

"What about me?" said Hunky Poole, hurrying up to Andy. "Want to shoot me out of a cannon?" It was a joke. Hunky had come to sneer, but now he too was caught up in the excitement.

Andy looked at Hunky and said gravely, "The elephants need a keeper. Would you like to work with the elephants?"

"No, no," said Georgie quickly, tugging at Andy's sleeve. "I can do that too."

"Her?" said Hunky, giving Georgie a withering look. "She's too small. Besides, she's a girl. Girls can't do elephants. I can, easy." Hunky thrust out his chest and clenched his fists.

"Oh, please," said Georgie, "let me."

But Andy looked soberly at Hunky, and said, "Well, all right, but you have to be gentle with elephants. You cannot just push them around."

"Well, naturally." Hunky snickered. "So what do I have to do? Teach them to stand on their heads?"

Andy paused, and glanced at Georgie, who looked unhappy. "Listen," he said to Hunky, "it is only necessary to keep them safe." He nodded at the pile of hay. "And of course they must be fed."

"Pretty stupid job, if you ask me," said Hunky. "Is that all I get to do?"

"No," said Andy. One of Otis's Indian clubs sailed past him, and he reached up and caught it. Laughing, he threw it back and said to Hunky, "There is something else very necessary and important."

"What's that?" said Hunky Poole.

"Cleaning up after them," said Andy.

27

THE MERRY-GO-ROUND

*T*HE MERRY-GO-ROUND was a surprise. It was right there beside the tent on Tuesday morning. A big, brightly colored sign ran around the canopy on top:

NOAH'S ARK

Noah's Ark! Georgie laughed. She remembered the police officers who had enjoyed the amazing document signed by Noah, that old man in the Bible story who built the ark and saved all the animals from the flood. The police officers would certainly be pleased!

And of course all the circus performers were thrilled

that their circus had its very own merry-go-round. Andy jumped up on the platform and shouted, "Come on, everyone! Please, you guys!"

With whistles and shrieks everybody jumped on board and climbed on the animals, and shouted *"Giddyup, horsie,"* and *"Ride 'im, cowboy!"*

But the wooden animals were not horses. All but two of them were wild creatures of the forest or beasts of the jungle—a lion, a tiger, an ostrich, a gorilla, a brown bear, a hippo, a giraffe, a moose and a wolf.

The other two were entirely different. They were extinct dinosaurs from some prehistoric age. One was a fat Brontosaurus with a long snaky neck. The other was Tyrannosaurus rex himself, towering above the rest.

All the animals from forest and jungle and both of the dinosaurs were beautifully carved and painted with rough fur or scales; broad antlers or long necks; sharp teeth or plump snouts; spots, stripes, or feathers.

"Ready?" shouted Andy, with his fingers on the switch.

There were cries of *"Let's go!"* and *"Yippee!"*

Oliver kicked the sides of Tyrannosaurus rex, Weezie Hoskins shrieked and grabbed her hippo by the ears, Frieda clung to the neck of her giraffe, Eleanor plumped herself down on the back of the ostrich, Cissie sat proudly on her moose as if it were a horse, Eddy clutched his tiger's wooden fur, Rachel put her arms around the neck of her Brontosaurus as far she could reach, Otis gripped his gray wolf with his legs, and Sidney tightened his arms around the wooden mane of his lion. By the time Hugo Von Bismarck clambered up on the platform, only the gorilla was left. Hugo crawled doubtfully up its sloping back and hung on.

Andy threw the switch. At once the platform started moving, the animals began plunging up and down and everybody screamed for joy.

Rising and falling and bounding forward and rising again, Georgie patted the powerful hump of her brown bear, just as if the creature were real.

But then she sucked in her breath and gasped, because the great beast turned its head to look at her and winked.

28

THE MISTERIOUS CIRCUS

*T*HE MERRY-GO-ROUND was glorious, the elephants were magnificent, and everybody was practicing hard, inspired by Andy—because it was Andy's circus, it was Andy's dream come true.

Rajah and Sita were old hands at marching. Mighty Rajah tramped heavily around the ring with Eleanor sitting gracefully on his head, and Sita followed Rajah, her trunk curled tightly around his tail.

Eddy's stilts were now *ten feet tall*; Sidney could mince along his wire three feet above the ground; Oliver's human pyramid was six kids high; Cissie could ride boldly around the ring kneeling on Maizie's back; Rachel had manufactured long strings of red, blue and yellow pennants; Otis could juggle three Indian clubs; Georgie could hang by her knees high in the air; and Oliver and Sidney had made up a crazy clown act.

Of course Weezie Hoskins was no help. Weezie was supposed to run errands for everybody else, but all she did was giggle and screech and get in the way.

Andy was busy all the time, giving pointers, improving everybody's act. He also worked on the circus tent, adding extra cables and guy wires to the tent poles and fastening the safety net to the poles with heavy knots. The wires and ropes sparkled with silver and gold, but they strengthened the net so that it would catch Georgie safely if she fell—but of course she couldn't possibly fall.

So far, so good. But for Grand Marshal Frieda it wasn't good enough.

Oh, it was all very well for Andy to do his fancy magic tricks, but why didn't he take charge? The trouble was, he was a dreamer, not a doer like Frieda. She could see that the circus would never really happen unless somebody got it all together. And that somebody was Frieda Caldwell.

She now had a clipboard for making lists. Frieda explained to Eddy the first item on the list. "Listen, Eddy, we've got to advertise the circus. Right away! We've got to tell everybody in town."

"Flyers," said Eddy wisely. "Ask Hugo. His father's a

big computer freak."

So early on Wednesday morning Frieda buttonholed Hugo Von Bismarck as his bicycle came bumping across the field. She grabbed him by the front of his shirt and nearly tipped him over. "Hey," said Hugo, "watch it."

But Frieda pushed back her top hat and looked at him sternly. "Hugo," she said, "we need flyers. A whole lot of flyers."

"Flyers?" he said, gaping at her. "What do you mean, flyers?"

Frieda handed him her clipboard, plucked a pencil from behind her ear and said, "Take this down."

Hugo was a big easygoing kid. He was bewildered, but he took the pencil and scribbled as fast as he could while Frieda invented the words of the flyer in her head and dictated them out loud. "Hold it," said Hugo. "You're going too fast."

Frieda slowed down. When she was finished, Hugo stared nervously at his scribbles, but Frieda reached for the clipboard, ripped out the page, handed it to him and said, "Okay, Hugo, now go home and print it out. Lots of flyers, Hugo. We need a couple of hundred flyers."

She had chosen the right man for the job. Hugo Von Bismarck might be a little slow in some ways and his spelling was certainly weird, but sitting at the keyboard of his father's computer, playing with all the widgets and thingamajigs, he was a whiz.

A couple of hours later he was back with his pile of printouts. Proudly he handed one to Frieda, expecting compliments and slaps on the back. His flyer looked like this:

Introducing

☉ THE ☉

!!! MISTERIOUS !!!

!!! CIRCUS !!!

!!! THE GREATEST SHOW ON EARTH !!!

PERFORMANCE TO BE ANNOUNCED!

Hugo looked expectantly at Frieda, but to his disappointment there was no praise, no slap on the back.

Her mouth had dropped open in horror. "Your spelling," she gasped. "It's all wrong."

"Oh, spelling," said Hugo. "Who cares about spelling?"

Dismayed, Frieda showed the flyer to Rachel, who was spreading out a long strip of cloth on the ground, a banner for the top of the tent. Rachel took one look and frowned. "It's spelled wrong," she said.

"Right," said Frieda, and at once she ran to show Andy.

But Andy only laughed and said the same thing as Hugo, "Who cares about spelling?"

And therefore, when the commuters of Concord drove home that afternoon past the circus grounds, they saw the banner floating high over the tent. Sidney and Eddy had slung it between two trees, and Rachel had copied Hugo's spelling exactly. The banner proclaimed:

!!! THE MISTERIOUS CIRCUS !!!
THE GREATEST SHOW ON EARTH

29

THE FLYING FLYERS

THE BANNER ON THE TENT was perfect—well, almost perfect—and the flyers were ready, but Frieda didn't know what to do next. Anxiously she said to Andy, "We've got to spread them all over town, but there aren't enough kids."

"We do not need kids," said Andy. "Watch this. No, wait just a moment." He looked around as if expecting a delivery truck to appear from behind a bush. But Eddy and Hugo could see nothing but a squirrel in a tree, Hugo's dusty bicycle and a couple of butterflies flapping up from a patch of daisies.

It seemed to be enough for Andy. He reached for Hugo's sheaf of flyers and tossed them carelessly over his head. At once they lifted and riffled apart and fluttered higher and higher, swooping like pigeons.

"Oh, I get it," said Hugo. "It's because they're flyers."

"Hey," said Eddy, "that's just so cool." Throwing back his head, he watched Hugo's flyers swarm together and pause, whirl uncertainly in a ring, and then take off toward the center of town.

Here on the ground the air was still, but up there a strong wind seemed to be blowing, because it was whipping the flyers high over Concord, swirling them around the church steeples and the flagpole, and fluttering them north, south, east and west.

Straining his eyes, Eddy could see the white flock thin and scatter. Hugo's flyers were drifting down like feathers over Walden Street and Main Street and Sudbury Road.

Rachel Adzarian happened to be shopping in the center of town with her mother when the flyers floated down, so she told everybody afterward what it had been like.

They had not fallen on the street like trash, Rachel said. Instead they had settled on porches and plastered themselves to front doors. On Main Street they had slapped against the door of the hardware store and smacked against the window of the bookshop. In the parking lot of the supermarket they had stuck to the windshields of cars.

Within the next half hour, every man, woman and child in Concord knew that something called

☉ THE ☉
!!! MISTERIOUS !!!
!!! CIRCUS !!!

had come to town and that it was

THE GREATEST SHOW ON EARTH!

and that its first performance was

TO BE ANNOUNCED!

30

THE GHASTLY MEETING

*T*HE SELECTMEN'S OFFICE IN the Town Hall had high windows, an American flag and a painting of the North Bridge—the famous bridge where the Minutemen had fought the British on the first day of the American Revolution.

And tremendous things had happened right here in the Town Hall. Uncle Freddy was always talking about Henry Thoreau's speech against the hanging of John Brown. Of course Henry was not here in the Town Hall today, but he was the subject of the meeting. Matilda MacIntosh made a motion:

Moved, that the Selectmen bring before a
Special Town Meeting a request for the funding

of a Henry Thoreau Theme Park in the Mill Brook meadow.

"But—but," spluttered Uncle Fred, "that's ridiculous. We can't bother the town with a crazy idea like that."

Matilda smiled at him sweetly. "But, Fred, dear, it's the democratic way. Surely the people of the town can decide for themselves."

"No, no," cried Uncle Fred, "not this time."

But Matilda's eyes were sparkling. Springing from her chair, she said, "Oh, my dear friends, I have wonderful news. Dizzy Enterprises—you've heard of Dizzy Enterprises? They are ready to begin work the instant the town gives the word."

"Begin work?" shouted Uncle Fred. "What do you mean, begin work?"

The poor man was behaving so badly! Matilda smiled at him. "Well of course there will have to be a little digging, a foundation for the cabin, that sort of thing."

Chairman Jerry Plummer looked at her nervously. "Cabin? What cabin?"

"My dear Jerry, this is a *Henry Thoreau Theme Park*. It will be *his* cabin, of course." Matilda leaned forward, beaming around the table, and whispered the heart and soul of her great idea. "And *he* will be there in person."

109

Uncle Freddy shot out of his chair. "*He?* Who do you mean, *he?*"

"Why, Henry himself, naturally. A motorized reproduction, life-size, six feet four inches tall."

"What?" Uncle Freddy gasped. "But Henry Thoreau wasn't six feet four inches tall!"

"Well, whatever," said Matilda. "Anyway, there he'll be in person, Henry Thoreau himself, to inspire the children of the nation with his remarks."

"Remarks?" croaked Uncle Fred. "How? How will he make remarks?"

"With buttons," explained Matilda with an angelic smile.

"What sort of buttons?" asked Jemima Smith, looking pale.

"On his coat, buttons to turn on the recordings. When a little child pushes a button, Henry will open his mouth and utter one of his little sayings."

"Little sayings!" shouted Uncle Fred.

Matilda closed her eyes in sorrow. Fred was making such a fool of himself. Turning to Chairman Plummer, she said sweetly, "Oh, Jerry, you have such a wonderful deep voice. You could be the living voice of Henry Thoreau."

"I could?" Chairman Plummer blushed and looked pleased.

"And, Annabelle, would you like to be Henry's wife?"

"But—" said Annabelle.

"Thoreau didn't have a wife," howled Uncle Fred.

"His sister then," said Matilda. "Wouldn't you like that, Annabelle? And Jemima, would you like to be the voice of Louisa May Alcott?"

Annabelle and Jemima looked dazzled.

"But, Jemima, you can't do it," bawled Uncle Fred. "Jerry, Annabelle, what are you thinking of?"

But Matilda had an ace up her sleeve. "Now, Fred," she cooed, "we need your wisdom most of all. You are the very one to choose Henry's remarks. Ten really inspiring remarks for the ten buttons on his shirt." She looked joyfully around the table. "Now, ladies and gentlemen, shall we take a vote?"

"No," shrieked Uncle Fred. "Over my dead body."

"Now, now, Fred," said Matilda, patting his shoulder as if he were a naughty boy, "I'm sure it won't come to that. Now listen, boys and girls, I forgot something. Just a little detail to be added to the motion."

She explained the little detail. Mesmerized, Chairman Plummer nodded his head up and down, apparently undismayed, and so did Jemima and Annabelle.

Uncle Fred was in a state of shock. The little detail was added and the vote was taken. It passed, four to one. The Thoreau Theme Park was on its way to Town

111

Meeting, and Dizzy Enterprises was to undertake a pilot project right away.

They would put up in the Mill Brook meadow a fiberglass cabin and a motorized figure, so that everybody in Concord would see what a blessing the theme park would be for the town.

And they would do it *before Town Meeting.*

31

THE ONE AND ONLY!

*T*HE MEETING WAS OVER. In despair, Uncle Fred staggered downstairs and almost tripped over the sill as he opened the door.

At once he looked up in surprise, because the air was full of white birds. No, not birds, they were pieces of paper, drifting down from the sky, tipping and floating, sailing left and right, darting here and there and zigzagging up and down.

The shower of paper was everywhere. Hugo's flyers for the Misterious Circus were floating down all over Monument Square.

As Uncle Fred stood frozen on the Town Hall steps, one of them skimmed sideways and aimed itself directly at his face, then poised in midair only a few inches in front of his nose as if begging him to read it.

But all he saw was the word *misterious* before Matilda MacIntosh came up behind him and snatched the piece of floating paper.

Matilda read it quickly, and then she looked up at the trees in Monument Square. They were all aflutter with flyers like white pigeons. She looked down at Lexington Road, where they were frolicking among the parked cars.

"Litter in the streets," cried Matilda MacIntosh. "It won't do." She looked at Fred Hall in triumph. "Those children of yours must be stopped." Then her tone changed, because the look on his face was so savage. "You know, Fred," she wheedled, "if Henry Thoreau were alive today, he'd be absolutely *thrilled* with my theme park."

"He would not," thundered Uncle Fred, but he was beaten and he knew it.

Stumbling home and opening the door of No. 40 Walden Street, he was comforted by the order in the front hall. Mrs. Truth was back on her newel post. Henry was settled comfortably in the curve of the stairs.

The wreckage had been repaired.

In his misery it occurred to Uncle Fred that although Henry would have despised the idea of a theme park in his honor, he might have been pleased to see the elephant. Had Henry ever seen an elephant? Probably not, but surely he would have liked it, because he had liked all natural creatures.

Uncle Fred put his hands on Henry's plaster shoulders and said, almost weeping, "You wouldn't be thrilled by the theme park, would you, Henry? Oh, Henry, I did my best, but I failed."

Aunt Alex came out of the schoolroom, brushing aside the velvet curtain.

"Oh, Fred dear, what's the matter?"

"The vote," groaned Uncle Fred. "That Matilda MacIntosh, she won the day. I told her the theme park would go to Town Meeting over my dead body." He sagged onto the wicker sofa. "Behold my dead body."

Aunt Alex was startled. "Matilda MacIntosh? She's a member of the board? It's her idea, the theme park? But she's my new—" Aunt Alex stopped in midsentence. The light had dawned.

"Right. She's a shark. She's Tyrannosaurus rex. She has everybody in her clutches. She's the boss of the world, the one and only."

So much for my new dearest friend, thought Aunt Alex bitterly. "Oh, Fred, you don't think it will pass Town Meeting?"

He smiled at her, looking hopeful. "No, of course

115

not. The people of Concord have more sense than to vote for a dumb thing like that."

But Aunt Alex wasn't so sure. She went outside to feed her chickens.

At once the banty rooster came bustling up, flapping his wings and pushing to the front. Aunt Alex leaned over the fence and scattered her cracked corn.

"Tell me, my lord," she said, "do you think you're the boss of the world?"

The little cock threw out his chest and crowed, *I do, I do, because I am! I'm the Great and Glorious Cock of the World! That's me, the one and only!*

Sighing, Aunt Alex looked up at the maple tree that hung over the chicken yard. All its leaves were nodding, brushing against each other and whispering.

What were they saying? *I am the leaf, the one and only?*

Never, decided Aunt Alex, grateful that something in the world was humble.

32

Cease and Desist!

*T*HE MIGHTY ARMORED TANK that was Matilda
MacIntosh was blundering powerfully forward
through the town of Concord, but her vow to
terminate the circus was still to be taken care of.

Arming herself with another official document, she
drove to the circus grounds and parked on Walden
Street. At once she was amazed by the gauzy tent, astonished by Rachel's bright flags and stunned by the noisy
merry-go-round. And then she couldn't believe her eyes
when a red-headed girl rode past her on the back of an
elephant much bigger than the one she had seen before.

And then Matilda gasped at a boy taking long strides
on high stilts and a girl standing up shakily on the broad

back of a horse. The girl teetered and leaned over to grasp the horse's mane, but then a grubby little kid ran up behind the horse and whacked its hindquarters with her skinny hand. At once the horse reared, the girl fell off and the scrawny little brat screeched with laughter.

But the girl wasn't hurt. Matilda watched, astonished, as Cissie dusted herself off and said, "Weezie, you little jerk," and climbed back up on the horse. "Hey, Andy, watch this," said Cissie, standing up bravely, not hanging on to anything this time, spreading out her arms like a real circus star.

"Go for it, Cissie," shouted the big kid on stilts and the girl on the elephant.

"Bravo, Cissie," said someone else. "I mean, that is truly cool."

Matilda turned and saw another boy. She had seen him before. Now she could see how important he was. He was the elephant boy. Her face changed, her eyes grew larger, she melted forward and said, "Oh, how do you do! My name is MacIntosh, but of course we met the other day. This time I have something for you, just a trifle." With an adorable smile, Matilda pulled a document out of her bag and handed it to the elephant boy.

It was an order demanding that they

CEASE AND DESIST!

The boy looked puzzled. "What does it mean, *cease and desist*?"

"It means stop," explained Matilda. "You are to stop all this foolishness at once."

"I see," said Andy politely, giving the document back. Then with a smile he reached up and plucked something out of the sky, or perhaps it had been hanging from the branch of a tree, or possibly it had popped up from behind a bush. He handed it to Matilda.

It was yet another parchment scroll, the perfect answer to her order to Cease and Desist:

To Whom It May Concern!

Festivals of Joy are hereby declared legal in both the Western and Eastern Hemispheres and at the North and South Poles. Any bylaw preventing such festivities is hereby overruled.

(signed)

Choirs of Angels

"That's ridiculous," said Matilda, but her eyes bulged. Tittering nervously, she dropped the document on the ground. "How utterly absurd," she said, stalking away. But then she looked back and added gaily, "Goodbye, you darling people. I'll be back."

119

"And she will, too," warned Eddie, jumping down from his stilts with a thud.

Matilda had said good-bye, but she didn't really leave the circus grounds. Instead she made a tour of inspection. Gliding around the tent, she saw a boy juggling Indian clubs, a girl painting a poster, another girl running after a toddler, a big kid lifting weights, and at last, all the way around on the other side of the tent, another elephant and a grouchy-looking boy.

It was Hunky Poole.

33

FRIEDA'S CLIPBOARD

EORGIE HAD BEEN AT home during the battle of the documents. She had not seen Matilda's order to Cease and Desist. She had not seen Andy's enchanted scroll about Festivals of Joy.

But she had been listening when Uncle Fred told Aunt Alex exactly what Dizzy Enterprises was planning to do in the Mill Brook meadow. She called Frieda's cell phone right away.

And of course Frieda took charge at once. "We've got to fight back," she told Georgie fiercely. "I'll put it on my agenda." She snatched up her clipboard. The only thing on her agenda so far was:

1. Everybody go home and make popcorn!

Now she scribbled:

2. Another flyer! Tell Hugo!
3. Council of war! Tell Andy!

It was the hottest day of the summer. No breeze stirred the bright new flags. They hung limp, and so did the long swaybacked sign for THE MISTERIOUS CIRCUS, THE GREATEST SHOW ON EARTH. The canopy of the merry-go-round sagged, the carved animals were not rising and falling as they often did in a light wind, and the gleaming fabric of the Big Top hung still.

But a lot was going on inside the tent just the same. Frieda stood out of the way as Rajah lumbered past her with Weezie Hoskins bouncing on his back, shrieking insanely. Rajah's great forehead was wrinkled as if he were unhappy.

There were *skreek*ing noises as Eddy's hammer clawed nails out of his stilts to make them even higher. Big Oliver and small Sidney were rehearsing their clown act—Sidney punched Oliver, and Oliver fell back and waggled his feet in the air. On the other side of the tent Cissie Updike was feeding her horse. Wisps of hay twitched and disappeared inside Maizie's jaw.

122

Beyond Cissie, Otis Fisher was practicing as usual. This time he had six Indian clubs in the air. He was trying to add one more, but he kept dropping it and starting over. Beside the center ring, Hugo sat at his command post fiddling with his electronic equipment, pushing a button to make the calliope start and stop. Shrill whistles puffed out of the pipes and then droned down the scale. The drums rattled and stopped and rattled again.

Frieda looked around. Where was Andy? Oh, there he was, working at something in the center ring. He was attaching the safety net even more tightly to the ringbolts in the tent poles. Frieda marched up to him and said severely, "Now listen here, Andy, the circus has got to save the meadow."

Andy finished his last knot and looked at her. "What meadow?"

"The Mill Brook meadow. Something horrible is happening."

She explained the whole thing, and Andy understood at once. "Oh, yes," he said, "that is indeed cool. We must work to save the meadow."

"So it's up to Hugo," said Frieda.

"Hugo?"

"Another flyer," said Frieda. "Hugo's got to make another flyer. And we've got to call a council of war."

"A what?"

"My whistle," said Frieda, fumbling in her pocket. "Where did I put my whistle?"

But then there was a scream from Weezie Hoskins, and they turned to see what was happening. Rajah, tired of her silliness, had reached up with his trunk, wrapped it around her, and set her on the ground. "Stupid old elephant," screeched Weezie, hopping up and down. Rajah moved ponderously up to Andy, who gave him a friendly slap on his towering side.

Frieda found her whistle, took a deep breath and blew a shrill blast.

34

FLYER NUMBER TWO

*H*UGO COULDN'T BELIEVE IT. "More flyers? You mean I gotta make another whole bunch of flyers?"

"Right," said Frieda. "And here's what they've got to say." Again she handed him her clipboard and began dictating slowly, with long sarcastic pauses between words, because Hugo kept saying, "Hold it."

Frieda loved dictating. When she was finished, she took the clipboard back from Hugo and corrected his spelling. She crossed out *Meddo* and wrote *Meadow*. She crossed out *Thorow* and wrote *Thoreau*.

"There you are, Hugo," she said briskly, tearing off the sheet of paper. "Now go home and get busy. We need three hundred new flyers by"—she looked at her Minnie Mouse watch—"three o'clock."

Hugo groaned, stuffed the paper in the front of his shirt, mounted his bicycle and rode grouchily away. He couldn't possibly turn out three hundred flyers by three o'clock.

But he did his best, and at three thirty he came wobbling back across the field on his bike with the three hundred new flyers in his backpack.

He handed them to Frieda, grinning. Once again he expected high praise, because the second set of flyers was even handsomer than the first.

ଚାଚାଚା

THE MISTERIOUS CIRCUS

JOINS THE FIGHT TO SAVE

THE MILL BROOK
!! MEADOW !!

!!! SAY NO TO
THE THOREAU THEME
!!! PARK !!!

ଚାଚାଚା

DOWN WITH METILDA MACINTOSH!!!

Hugo had added the last sentence on his own. Frieda was horrified. "But, Hugo, you can't put things like that on a sign. Go back and do it over."

"Do it over!" Hugo couldn't believe his ears. He looked pleadingly at Andy, but Andy had snatched his juggling balls out of his shirt and he was tossing them higher and higher—silver ones, gold ones, sky-blue ones— up they went, a dozen of them, all in the air at once.

"But all that paper," whined Hugo. "My pop will have a fit."

Andy caught the little balls deftly and put all of them away in his shirt except for one of the silver ones, which he handed to Hugo. "This should take care of the expense," he said kindly.

Astonished, Hugo looked at his hand. It was full of silver dollars.

"Oh, well, okay, I guess," he said, putting them in his pocket. They were so heavy, they pulled his pants down on that side. Wearily he picked up his bicycle again and bumped away, his shoulders sagging.

At home in his father's study, Hugo deleted the line about Matilda MacIntosh, but then there was an empty space at the bottom. He looked over the display of computer widgets and thingamajigs, chose one, and ran it across the empty space. It looked fine.

Then the printer took a long time to turn out three hundred copies, and Hugo had to keep feeding in more paper. But within the hour he was back at the circus grounds with the second set of flyers.

Frieda read one of them and said crossly, "Hugo, what are all those boats doing down there at the bottom?"

Hugo said nothing, but when Frieda looked up and saw his face, she said, "Well, they're okay, I guess."

Hugo spoke up in a funny Frieda-like voice, "And thanks a *bushel*, dear Hugo."

Frieda wasn't stupid. "Oh, yes, of course, Hugo, thanks a lot. I mean, you've contributed just *incredibly* to the whole agenda." She looked sideways at Andy. "Right, Andy?"

"Oh, yes," said Andy, "that is right."

"Good old Hugo," said Eddy, clapping him on the back.

Then Frieda and Hugo and Eddy watched Andy pick up handful after handful of the new flyers and toss them over his head. Once again they flew up like birds, whirled aloft by a breeze that had sprung up just in time.

"I don't see how you do that," said Eddy, watching the flyers flutter up and take off for the center of town.

"I don't either," said Hugo, gaping at the sky. "I mean, it's like you get these hot tips from the weatherman."

"Oh, well," said Andy as he hurled up another batch,

128

"there's really nothing to it. You know the way a butterfly flaps its wings in China and starts a little breeze? And then the breeze turns into a wind and pretty soon there's a storm over the ocean? That's all it is."

"But I don't see—," said Eddy.

"Oh, I get it," said Hugo. "It's just some butterfly way over there in China." And he went away satisfied.

35

MATILDA STRIKES BACK

W HEN HUGO'S NEW PRINTOUTS showered down over the town of Concord, Matilda MacIntosh was far away in New York City in the offices of Dizzy Enterprises.

She had not waited for the vote by the selectmen. Weeks ago Matilda had started the theme park moving. Now on the fifty-fourth floor of the Dizzy Tower, she leaned across the desk of the project manager and said, "I just want to see how my pilot project is coming along. I can hardly wait."

"Your pilot project?" The project manager shuffled his papers. "Oh, right, you mean that little thing in Concord." He smiled at Matilda. "I am happy to inform you that it has already been packaged. It is in the truck. It is on its way."

"How thrilling!" said Matilda.

Therefore she missed Frieda's call to arms. But a few days later she found Hugo's second flyer in her backyard, fluttering in a lilac bush. She plucked it off and read it. How absurd! What did those little kids think they could do against the power and might of the Concord Board of Selectmen and the upcoming vote in Town Meeting?

Then Matilda nodded wisely, standing there in the sunshine beside the lilac bush. Oh, well, of course, this was Fred Hall's doing. It was his little brats who were behind that silly circus. Cousin Ralph had been right. Those Halls were troublemakers, the entire family. "Even their kittycats," snickered Matilda.

Then she reminded herself that one of the circus kids, at least, was on her side. A couple of twenty-dollar bills had persuaded the boy to help out. He had sworn to think of something.

She tossed the nonsensical flyer away, but at once it flapped back and stuck to her face. And then she couldn't get rid of it. Every time she pulled it off, it flew back and plastered itself on her nose. At last Matilda managed to crumple it into a ball and drop it in the trash can. Then as she slammed down the lid, she thought of a new plan.

She would go to the press. She would attack that stupid circus on the front page of the local paper.

Next day, there it was, the headline in the *Concord Weekly*, right under the article about Town Meeting:

DOES CIRCUS ENDANGER CHILDREN OF CONCORD?

Selectwoman MATILDA MACINTOSH Expresses Concern

"She may be right," said Aunt Alex, looking at the headline and shaking her head.

"Nonsense," said Uncle Fred, but he was worried too. And he was unhappy about something strange that had turned up overnight in the field across the street.

A large object wrapped in black plastic had been dumped in the middle of the Mill Brook meadow. A *thing*. What was it?

36

THE *THING*

MATILDA MacINTOSH DIDN'T hear about the *thing* until the driver of the flatbed delivery truck and his buddy from Dizzy Enterprises called her from a fast-food place in New Haven.

"Miz MacIntosh? Ma'am? Your item,"—the truck driver looked at his slip—"order number 876204777B— has been deposited on-site."

At once Matilda jumped into her car and drove to Heywood Street. Yes, there it was, she could see it from the car window—a bulky black cube in the middle of the field.

She hopped out and scrambled down into the meadow. In her hurry she blundered too near the Mill

Brook, and one of her feet sank into the muddy bank. She pulled it out and flapped her sopping skirt. Then, with one shoe squelching at every step, she hurried across the meadow through a tangle of blackberry canes and wildflowers to the place where the bulky black object loomed above her in the field—her gift-wrapped present from Dizzy Enterprises. Oh, what would she find inside?

The bulky object was silent, keeping its secret.

Matilda fumbled in her purse for a pair of scissors. It took only a few minutes to snip the strings, slash the tape and pull away the wrapping to reveal Henry's fiberglass cabin in all its glory.

Oh, it was charming! The shingles looked so real, and the aluminum chimney had been painted to resemble bricks, and the plastic door was molded to look like boards.

Eagerly Matilda pushed the doorbell. At once a chime tinkled inside the cabin. Then she stood back and watched Henry's door swing slowly open.

There he was in person: Henry Thoreau himself.

Matilda clasped her hands in wonder as the fiberglass dummy glided out on invisible wheels and jerked its arm in greeting. It was six feet tall, pink-cheeked and handsome. The Dizzy artist had copied the face of Derek Cherniak, Matilda's favorite TV star. And she herself had

134

ordered his clothes from L.L. Bean, his grouse-shooting coat and barnyard shirt, his down-Maine pants and Green Mountain hiking boots.

They were just right for this country yokel who had written a book. And his gears were working smoothly. Matilda was delighted to see Henry's mechanical chin move up and down, and she was thrilled to hear the scratchy words that came out of his fiberglass mouth.

"Hi there!" boomed the loudspeaker inside the fiberglass head. "Welcome to my cabin! My name is Henry! What's yours?"

Oh, he was perfect! "My name's Matilda," giggled Matilda. And then she waited for Henry to say something else. The grinning mouth was wide open, but nothing more came out.

Oh, of course, she had forgotten the buttons. Yes, there they were on Henry's shirt, all ten of them. Matilda pushed the top button, and at once Henry opened his mouth and squawked, "Old shoes." Then there was a click and a metallic buzz, and he said it again, "Old shoes."

Was that all? Henry's mouth was still half open, but the recording seemed to be stuck. Matilda was puzzled. Old shoes? Why was he talking about old shoes?

She tried the second button, but all it did was buzz. The third one squealed. The rest were silent. They hadn't been digitally programmed, and Matilda soon guessed why. The crew from Dizzy Enterprises didn't know anything about Henry Thoreau, that was the trouble. What a pity that Fred Hall had refused to choose Henry's remarks himself!

Well, it was okay. She would find somebody else to do it. There were plenty of Thoreau freaks in the town of Concord. After all, you couldn't pick up a rock around here without finding a bunch of those crazies squirming around below.

So now there were three Henrys in the town of Concord. One was Matilda MacIntosh's fiberglass dummy. The second was Uncle Freddy's plaster bust. And the third was the ghost of Henry himself, which was everywhere—in rabbits in thorny tangles and woodchucks in their holes, in geese squawking over Nine Acre Corner, in deer crashing through ferny thickets, in muskrats in the river and trout in Walden Pond, in the bright fleets of orange butterflies that fluttered among the milkweed flowers in Concord fields, and in the sparkling water of the narrow stream that ran through the Mill Brook meadow.

And also perhaps in a dozen Concord kitchens where kids were popping corn.

37

THE ROTTENNESS OF HUNKY POOLE

WHILE MATILDA MACINTOSH rejoiced in the birth of her theme park, the circus kids were working harder than ever.

Otis had mastered his Indian clubs. He could keep seven in the air at once. Cissie could stand up gracefully on the broad back of her horse, leaning a little inward to keep her balance while Maizie plodded around the ring. Cissie's little brother Carrington was now the squealing pinnacle of a seven-kid human pyramid. Oliver Winslow's enormous feet were spread wide at the bottom, Hugo sat on his mighty shoulders, Sidney sat on Hugo's, Eleanor on Sidney's, Rachel on Eleanor's, Frieda on Rachel's, Weezie on Frieda's and Carrington on Weezie's.

Cissie had her doubts about Weezie. "I don't know if we should trust her with Carrington," she said to Oliver. "She's such an itchy little kid."

But Weezie was not about to make trouble high in the air, because it was too scary up there. Strangling Frieda with her skinny legs, she gripped Carrington's chubby ankles with all the scrawny muscles in her fists.

Georgie worried about all the leftover elephants in her pocket. There were ten of them left in the little red seed. She took it out and showed it to Andy in the palm of her hand. "Do you want another one, Andy?"

He shook his head. "Not yet, Georgie. Later on."

So Georgie put the seed away again, proud to have ten great creatures folded so secretly in her pocket. Then she and Andy climbed the ladder to the top of the tent and sat down side by side on the trapeze. It was time for a lesson in falling.

Andy knew exactly what to do, because he had seen it so many times whenever the Mexican circus came to Bangalore. It looked perfectly simple. "You just fall straight down," he told Georgie. "Feet first with your arms folded." He stood up and said, "Like this," and fell into empty air.

Georgie watched as he plummeted straight down and bounced on the springy net. At once he wallowed to the edge and somersaulted to the ground.

138

But before climbing up again, Andy tugged at the knotted ropes fastening the net to the poles on either side. "Good," he said. "They would hold an elephant." Swiftly he ran back up the ladder, sat down beside Georgie and said, "Do you wish to try?"

Georgie gripped the ropes and stood up, not at all afraid, remembering with longing the way it had felt to slip off the back of the great bird called the Goose Prince, on those beautiful moonlit nights two summers ago when they had flown together over Walden Pond. "Yes, yes," she said eagerly, "I want to try."

"Good," said Andy, but then there was an angry shout from below.

It was Hunky Poole. "Hey, you up there," he roared at Andy. "I've had it with elephant poop."

Andy sighed, and called, "Wait a moment. I will come down."

But Georgie touched his arm and said quickly, "I'll take care of the elephants. Let me."

"No, no," said Andy, "your job is right here," and he climbed down the ladder to talk to Hunky. From her high perch Georgie could see them arguing, Andy explaining, Hunky shaking his fist.

She could also see Eddy approaching on his lofty stilts. His head was so high, he could almost reach out and touch her, but he had to keep gripping the tops of his stilts, so he only nodded and grinned at Georgie.

But Hunky saw him coming, and he shouted at Andy, "Why don't you make *him* take care of the elephants?" With a sudden lunge, Hunky flung out a leg and tripped one of Eddy's stilts, and Eddy came crashing down.

He had not been trained in falling, and there was no net to catch him. He struck the ground headfirst. Hunky scuttled away and Georgie scrambled down the ladder.

But Eddy was sitting up, groaning and holding his head. Andy knelt beside him and felt his arms and legs, murmuring, "I think he is all right."

But a purple lump was bulging over Eddy's right ear. He spoke up thickly, bringing terrible curses down on the head of his old enemy, Harold "Hunky" Poole.

As for Hunky himself, he had a favorite hiding place outside where no one could see him cry.

38

THE HORRIBLE TOWN
MEETING

*T*HE SPECIAL TOWN MEETING was next day.
To Matilda MacIntosh it was almost too late. Only a few of her best friends had been given a chance to see the pilot project of the Henry Thoreau Theme Park.

Late in the afternoon of the day before Town Meeting, while the last rays of the setting sun shone golden on the water of the Mill Brook, Matilda and three other members of the board of selectmen stood in front of the pilot project. "Isn't it wonderful?" said Matilda. "Aren't you stunned?"

They were stunned, all right. Annabelle Broom said

feebly, "How nice." Jerry Plummer and Jemima Smith were speechless.

Of course the family across the road at No. 40 Walden Street had seen it, and so had Andy and all the kids from the circus. The kids were too young to vote, but Frieda stamped into her house and commanded her parents to do the right thing at Town Meeting.

"Mom! Dad!" cried Rachel to Mr. and Mrs. Adzarian. "You can't let the other guys win."

Hugo said "Hey, Pop," to his father, and Mr. Von Bismarck, looking at the mess of waste paper in his study, groaned and said okay.

"Mom," said Cissie, "listen to me. This time you've got to get with it."

Andy looked anxiously at Professor and Mrs. Hall, but Eddy said, "Cool it, Andy. Don't worry."

Cool it? Andy was puzzled. What did *cool it* have to do with *being cool*?

And of course Otis, Sidney and Oliver hollered at their mothers and fathers. But all the circus mothers and fathers in town were not enough, because the rest of the town was swept away.

It was incredible. Why didn't they see the ghastliness of a Henry Thoreau Theme Park in the Mill Brook meadow? But there were only a few objections.

Sidney's father wasted his time at the microphone

by trying to read from Henry Thoreau's book. He kept flipping the pages and saying, "No, that's not it," and he dropped the book twice. Professor Von Bismarck was next. He strode to the front of the hall, waved away the microphone and gave a speech that nobody could hear. Mrs. Caldwell took a turn at the microphone, reading a fiery statement dictated by her daughter Frieda.

And of course selectman Frederick Hall did his passionate best, but then Matilda MacIntosh rose grandly from her chair.

Holding the mike close to her face like a rock star, Matilda smiled broadly around the hall and said, "Of course, every member of the board is free to give an opinion. We all know the sincerity of Fred's belief, although it is just *possible* that he objects to the theme park because it will be right across the street from his own house."

Aha, a selfish motive! Uncle Fred's jaw dropped. Looking around, he could see people nodding their heads and grinning.

Matilda plunged on. "But you should know that the rest of the board voted for the theme park." She turned to the row of pale faces behind her. "Jerry?" she said, beaming at him. "Annabelle? Jemima?" At once all eyes turned expectantly to Jerry Plummer, Jemima Smith and Annabelle Broom.

Their faces were blank. For a long moment they just sat there. But then Jemima Smith bobbed up for a split second, muttered something, and plumped herself down.

Staring at the ceiling, Jerry Plummer shambled out of his chair, said faintly, "It's okay with me, I guess," and flopped down again.

Annabelle Broom reminded herself firmly that she was Matilda's best friend, but she too stayed on her feet for only a second. So it wasn't exactly a chorus of cheers.

But it was enough. All that remained was Matilda's speech, which she had saved for last. Matilda had three points to make:

1. The theme park will teach the children of Concord about their sublime heritage.
2. It will teach that glorious heritage to tourists from all over the world.
3. It will bring in so much money that taxes will fall to almost nothing.

Half the people in the auditorium were asleep, but the rest were spellbound as Matilda finished her speech and cried, "Mr. Moderator, I call for the vote."

"No, no," shouted Uncle Fred, jumping from his chair, "not yet!"

But the moderator's gavel came down with a bang, and the vote was taken. Six hundred twenty-one citizens stood up to vote for the Henry Thoreau Theme Park. Only twenty-nine voted against it.

"The motion is passed," boomed the moderator.

At once Matilda held up her hand and warbled, "I move to adjourn the meeting."

"So moved," bellowed the moderator. "All in favor say aye."

"AYE," cried six hundred and twenty-one citizens of Concord, standing up and shuffling into the aisles, eager to go home to bed.

"I can't understand it," said Aunt Alex, walking out the door with Uncle Fred. "How could they vote that way, all those good people?"

"They were mesmerized," said Uncle Fred. Grimly he repeated a wise old saying. "You can fool some of the people all of the time and all of the people some of the time. I guess this is one of the times."

"Right," said Aunt Alex angrily, "but I just can't stand it."

They were waiting at the door—Eddy, Eleanor, Georgie and Andy. They didn't have to ask what had happened. They could see it in Aunt Alex's face and Uncle Fred's drooping shoulders.

The Town Meeting had been a disaster.

39

EDDY'S PANTS

NEXT DAY THE PERFORMERS dragged themselves to the circus grounds. Most of them were lugging bags of homemade popcorn. Even the elephants seemed to know what had happened at Town Meeting. Gloomily Sita and Rajah shuffled their feet.

But Frieda clapped on her top hat, stood on a chair, blew her whistle, and shouted, "The show must go on." Then she began ordering everybody around. "Hugo, go home and make a flyer."

"Another flyer?" gasped Hugo.

"Right. So people know when to come." She snapped open her clipboard and handed him the script. "Like it's next Saturday at noon. And, hey, Hugo, how about the command post? You got that all set?"

"Oh, jeez no, not yet," moaned Hugo.

"Clowns," cried Frieda, "Have you got your mops?"

"Mops?" said Sidney.

"Whaddayamean, mops?" said Oliver.

"Floor mops. You know, Oliver, for funny clown wigs. Cissie, where's your red coat? And, hey, where's Rachel? Listen, Rachel, get busy and make Otis a handlebar mustache. Otis—" Frieda couldn't think what to tell Otis, because he was perfect already. "Eleanor, how about some sparkles?"

"Sparkles?" whimpered Eleanor. "What do you mean, sparkles?"

"Like you glue them all over your tutu. Georgie, have you got any pink tights?"

Even Andy was commanded to find a costume. "Look, Andy," said Frieda, "you have to look like a maharajah."

"A maharajah?" said Andy, aghast.

"You know, in baggy pants."

Then Frieda looked at her clipboard and frowned at Eddy. "And listen, Eddy, you need long pants for your stilts. You know, just incredibly long pants. Weezie Hoskins, what do you think you're doing? Weezie, get lost."

They went off in all directions, obeying orders. Eddy went home and said, "Hey, Aunt Alex, I need a pair of pants. You know, for my stilts."

147

"For your stilts?" said Aunt Alex. "Well of course, Eddy. I'll add a few inches to your school pants."

"No, no, Aunt Alex," said Eddy. "They've got to be really long."

"How long?"

"Oh, about fifteen feet," guessed Eddy. "With a drawstring at the top. You know."

"Fifteen feet! Your stilts aren't that long, are they, Eddy?" Aunt Alex was horrified. "What if you fall?"

"Don't worry, Aunt Alex," said Eddy proudly. "It's a snap. There's nothing to it."

Doubtfully Aunt Alex got to work. She pulled down the curtains in the sitting room and sewed them end to end.

Far into the night she cut and pinned, then bowed over the sewing machine. Eleanor came downstairs at midnight. "Let me help, Aunt Alex."

"Oh, thank you, Eleanor dear. Here, you can pin the other leg."

Comfortably they worked together. Aunt Alex's machine buzzed and Eleanor jabbed pins into the seams.

When the pants were finished, Aunt Alex stretched them out on the floor and looked at them—they were so long!—and said gravely, "Tell me, Eleanor, do you think Eddy's stilts are dangerous?"

"Oh no, Aunt Alex," said Eleanor, jumping up and

heading for the stairs. "They're not dangerous at all. You don't need to worry." This was a fib, of course, but it was important not to upset Aunt Alex. What if she or Uncle Fred or some other anxious grown-up called everything to a halt?

Eddy's long pants were a huge success. They made his long stilts look just like long legs. Andy and Georgie had perfected their trapeze act. Andy hung by his knees, swinging back and forth. Georgie sprang from her trapeze with her arms stretched out, and he caught her in midair. The net was there below them, but they didn't need it. They were a perfect team.

On Wednesday, Eleanor and Hunky Poole watched the trapeze act while they stuffed bag after bag with popcorn. "They're really good," said Eleanor. "But I'm glad the net is there. You know, just in case."

"Oh, sure," said Hunky. Abandoning the popcorn, he wandered over to inspect the knots that attached the net to the tent poles, remembering the lady who had been so nice to him, the one who had patted his arm and given him a couple of twenty-dollar bills. She had smiled at him so sweetly and then she had said, "I know you'll think of something, a clever boy like you!"

Hunky made up his mind, but his heart thumped in his chest.

40

THE LAST FLYER

HUGO'S NEW FLYERS were the best yet. All three
hundred were in glorious color. Frieda looked
at them and said, "Hugo, it's a masterpiece."

!!! THE MISTERIOUS CIRCUS !!!

!!!!! FIRST THRILLING PERFORMANCE !!!!!

◊ ◊ ◊

COME ONE COME ALL

!!! NEXT SATURDAY 2 PM !!!

WALDEN STREET CIRCUS GROUNDS

◊ ◊ ◊ ◊ ◊ ◊ ◊

CLOWNS! JUGGLERS! ACROBATS!

ELEPHANTS!!!! ELEPHANTS!!!! ELEPHANTS!!!!

"Gee, thanks," said Hugo proudly. "But my dad's gonna skin me alive when he finds out I used up all his color cartridges. And, hey, Frieda, I dunno about all those elephants, down there at the bottom. It looks like we've got thousands of elephants, but there's only Rajah and Whatsername."

"It's just poetic license," said Frieda.

"What kind of license is that?" said Hugo.

But Frieda was rushing off to find Andy, because he was the only one who had the trick of tossing up the flyers so they'd be caught by the breeze and fly all over town. He was like a baseball player with a special pitch, or a golfer with a powerful swing.

Matilda MacIntosh made a triumphant call to the project manager at Dizzy Enterprises to tell him they now had a green light to go ahead.

They could begin work right away on the whole vision of the entire concept of the actual manifestation of the Henry Thoreau Theme Park in the Mill Brook meadow.

The project manager was willing, but he sounded a little scornful. "Your theme park is so trivial," he said. "Most of our parks are as big as small towns. We cut down forests and dig artificial lakes; we build fairy castles and fiberglass cathedrals. Your little park is hardly worth our trouble."

"But it's so important!" cried Matilda.

"Well, okay, we'll get to work on it. Nothing to it. Coupla bulldozers, that's all we'll need—two or three heavy-duty dump trucks, front-end-loader, cement mixer, ripping machine, maybe a sixty-foot crane."

"How thrilling!" said Matilda MacIntosh.

41

A Little Touch of Hunky in the Night

*H*UNKY POOLE HAD CLEANED up after his last elephant.

On Friday afternoon everybody went home for supper, tired and excited about tomorrow. Hunky stayed behind and said good-bye to the elephants by giving the small one a kick in the backside. At once the big one wrapped his trunk around Hunky and threw him down.

Scrambling to his feet, Hunky shook his fist at Rajah. Then he backed timidly away and wandered around the circus grounds, dodging into the big tent to help himself to one of the bags of popcorn. Dodging out again, he found his hiding place near the merry-go-round and settled down to wait for darkness. Huddling in the bushes, he worked his way through the bag of popcorn, wondering why everybody hated him. Even the elephants hated Hunky. It felt terrible to be hated.

Why didn't Eddy Hall ever stop him in school and say, "Hey, Hunky, why don't you come over?" Why didn't Sidney Bloom ever yell at him, "Hey, Hunky, where'd you get that great T-shirt?" Why didn't Hugo Von Bismarck ever punch his arm and shout, "Hey, Hunky, whaddayasay?"

If those guys would only talk to him like that, everything would be okay. But they never did.

Night was a long time coming. At last Hunky decided it was dark enough. He crept past the merry-go-round and aimed his flashlight at the silent animals—the painted lion and the striped tiger and the Tyrannosaurus rex. They all seemed to scowl at him as he scuttled by, as if they hated him too. And there were faint squealings and strange growlings. A shiver ran down Hunky's spine. It was like those dumb animals wanted to jump down and pounce on poor old Hunky Poole.

Cowed and afraid of the dark, Hunky plunged inside the circus tent. Sweeping his flashlight this way and that, he began to look around.

42

COME ONE, COME ALL!

"TIME TO GO," said Uncle Fred. "Look at all those people heading down the road! If we don't hurry, all the seats will be gone."

"Oh, I'll be so glad when it's over," said Aunt Alex, running down the stairs. Uncle Fred pushed open the screen door, and together they hurried down the porch steps.

But just as they reached the gate, the telephone rang.

Hugo's flyer had done the trick. Crowds of people were coming from all over town to see the clowns, jugglers, acrobats and elephants.

And it wasn't just families with small children. A lot

155

of older kids came too, because school had started in late August and Oliver Winslow had slapped up Hugo's flyers all over the high school, and Eleanor Hall had given a sales talk over the public address system, and her brother Eddy had badgered all the ninth graders into coming. Some of the twelfth graders snickered at the idea of a little kids' circus, but most of them came anyway, grinning and shrugging their shoulders.

But there were old people too. A nursing home sent a whole busload of elderly folks to see the cute little children with rosy cheeks.

Attracting customers to the merry-go-round, Noah's Ark, was Sidney Bloom's job. "Come one, come all," shouted Sidney as the families poured out of their cars. And then of course all the little kids tugged their mothers and fathers to the merry-go-round, and whole families climbed up onto the platform and the mothers and fathers held their little tots on the backs of the toy animals, and one of the mothers said, "My goodness, it really is like Noah's Ark."

Sidney pushed the button, and the little tots went around and around and up and down, crowing with joy, and a few of the older kids jumped up on the Tyrannosaurus and the Brontosaurus and went around too, whooping and hollering.

Then there was the sound of a whistle blast, and

everybody headed for the Big Top. On her way in, Annabelle Broom fingered the gossamer cloth and said, "What is it made of? It's just like chiffon."

"No, not chiffon," said Dorothy Plummer. "It's more like organdy."

"Or maybe satin," said Marigold Brisket.

"No, no," said Jemima Smith, "I know what it is. It's swansdown."

But Aunt Alex had recognized it from the beginning because she had seen it before. It was the same as the delicate tissue of the wedding gown in the attic. The beautiful dress had always been hidden under a sheet, but one day when Aunt Alex and Eleanor were up there together, Eleanor had lifted the covering. "It's the snowflake wedding dress," she had told Aunt Alex. "Aunt Lily wore it when she married Prince Krishna."

"Snowflakes! That's impossible," Aunt Alex had said.

"Look," said Eleanor. She had held up one of the sleeves so that Aunt Alex could see that every tiny part of the lacy fabric was different from every other part. "Just like snowflakes, you see, Aunt Alex."

Now, inside the tent, the snowflake walls soared up and up, billowing slightly in puffs of air from the pipes of the calliope.

Hugo at his command post had everything to think about at once. The buttons for the calliope were on his switchboard. Now he turned the dial up to full volume, and "Yankee Doodle" began tooting and crashing and banging so loud, you couldn't hear yourself think. The calliope engine whined, and one belt whizzed up and the other whirled around, and the squeezebox whistled *wheezity-wheeze*, the horns blared *tootely-toot*, the drumsticks pounded *rat-a-tat-tat* and the cymbals clashed *clangity-clang*.

It made a tremendous racket. Little kids shrieked with excitement, fathers roared, "Calm down," mothers laughed and held their hands over their ears, and popcorn flew in all directions.

There were only three rows of seats in the big circle around the ring.

Aunt Alex and Uncle Fred sat down in the top row and looked around.

There was no sign of Eddy or Eleanor or Georgie. In fact, nobody was in sight except Eddy's friend Hugo, who was almost hidden behind some sort of electronic gadget. They couldn't see Hugo's wrinkled forehead. They didn't know he was frantic with worry. Poor Hugo was supposed to buzz Frieda whenever he thought it was time to start, and it was a huge responsibility.

Then Uncle Freddy nudged Aunt Alex, because Frieda in her top hat was peering out of an opening on the other side of the tent. Beside her a long gray trunk swayed as if smelling the air, and then withdrew.

Outside the tent Frieda got to work at once, lining everybody up for the grand parade. She herself would be first in line, of course, strutting along in her top hat with her whistle in her teeth. Eddy would be next, striding along on his stilts, and then the two clowns, Oliver and Sidney, in their wig mops, followed by Otis tossing up his Indian clubs. Cissie and her horse Maizie would be next, and then Andy on his unicycle. The two elephants would bring up the rear—Georgie and Weezie on Sita, and Eleanor in her spangled tutu on Rajah, with Carrington on her lap.

"Okay, okay," said Frieda, walking up and down the line, "the important thing is *timing*. No gaps! Something's got to happen every minute. Is everybody ready?" She gazed up at Eddy on his high stilts. "Ready, Eddy?"

Eddy pretended to wobble and save himself, and Frieda gasped. Then he grinned down at her. "Sure, I'm ready."

"Ready, Otis?"

"You bet," said Otis, tossing up an Indian club and catching it behind his back.

"Ready, clowns?"

"Watch this," said Oliver, because he and Sidney had an act. Now they reared back, glared at each other, snatched off each other's red noses and stuck them on

159

their own faces. They were hilarious.

"Well, okay, okay," said Frieda, hurrying on to Andy, who promptly pedaled around her on his unicycle. "All set, Andy?"

Andy was so excited, he could hardly speak. He whispered, "All set."

"Eleanor? Are you and Carrington okay?"

High on Rajah's back, Eleanor posed like a beauty queen and grinned at Frieda, and Carrington bounced on her lap in his little clown suit.

"You all right too, Rajah?" said Frieda, patting his gray trunk. Rajah curled it around her in a gentle hug, and then Frieda went on to Sita at the end of the parade.

"You okay, Georgie?" said Frieda, beaming up at her, because they were best friends. Georgie beamed back at Frieda and nodded. Yes, she was ready.

"Well, okay then, everybody," shouted Frieda through her megaphone. "Wait for the buzzer."

But first Andy walked his unicycle back to the end of the line and called up to Georgie, "It's time now, Georgie."

"Oh, yes," said Georgie. At once she pulled the red seed out of the pocket of her short spangled skirt and handed it down.

"Thank you," said Andy. And then as Hugo's buzzer sounded, he pulled out the stopper.

43

TEN GREAT KINGS AND QUEENS

*I*N THE MEANTIME, as the circus parade began under the Big Top and "Yankee Doodle" shrieked and whistled out of the calliope, terrible things were happening in the Mill Brook meadow.

The machines were arriving. The first of the bull-dozers lumbered down into the field, wallowing and tipping, landing with a rattling crash and thundering forward.

The ground shook, the cabin trembled and a few plastic shingles fell off the roof. Then the door-opening apparatus went haywire, and the fiberglass dummy began rolling violently forward, bashing its nose and rolling back and then whizzing forward again until it slammed against the door so hard that the hinges burst and the door fell flat. At once the dummy popped out into the fresh air squawking, "Old shoes! Old shoes!"

But the noise and vibration did not reach as far as the circus grounds. In the big tent half a mile away, all ears were deafened by the tremendous noise of the calliope as a pint-sized grand marshal made a majestic entrance in her silk top hat.

Frieda lifted her megaphone and shouted:

WELCOME TO THE MISTERIOUS CIRCUS, THE GREATEST SHOW ON EARTH!

Then her whistle shrieked and she began strutting around the ring, followed by Eddy on his lofty stilts. There were cheers and whistles. Aunt Alex gasped, but Uncle Fred only laughed and said, "So that's where those curtains went." Everybody clapped and waved, and there was a snowstorm of flying popcorn.

Sidney and Oliver were next, bouncing around in their clown suits, snatching off each other's red noses and wig mops. Then Oliver had the bright idea of clapping his wig down on the bald head of a man in the front row. The man grinned like a good sport, and everybody screamed with laughter.

It was a new funny thing to do. Oliver and Sidney

pranced sideways all the way around the ring, plastering noses and wigs on one little kid after another, with waves of laughter following them all the way.

Otis Fisher was a big hit too, tossing his Indian clubs high overhead and catching them expertly, sometimes in front, sometimes in back. When his handlebar mustache fell off, he tossed it up with the rest. Otis was a scream.

When everybody laughed, he was so thrilled that he thought of another funny trick on the spur of the moment. His Indian clubs went crazy. Otis ran around letting some of them drop on his head—*bonkity bonk*—and the rest of them bounce on the ground. Then while everybody clapped wildly, he gathered all his Indian clubs together, tossed them high, caught them all perfectly, and bowed in all directions while everybody shrieked and clapped and the high school kids whistled through their teeth.

No gaps! Frieda had said. *Something has to happen every minute!*

Therefore Cissie was ready. While Otis was finishing his act and making his bows, she urged Maizie into the ring and began trotting in a circle, sitting comfortably astride in her smart riding pants, velvet hat and red coat. Her feet were bare.

Then Frieda shouted into her megaphone:

163

LADEEZ AND GENTLEMEN, PLEASE WELCOME THE EQUESTRIAN WONDER OF THE WORLD, OUR OWN CISSIE UPDIKE!

Cissie sprang to her feet and stood upright while Maizie loped around the ring. There were gasps of astonishment.

Could this really be Cissie Updike, that funny little kid in the sixth grade? Hurray for Cissie! They clapped and clapped.

Then everything began to happen at once. As soon as Cissie plumped herself down again on Maizie's back, Sidney started to prance across his high wire six feet above the ground, balancing himself with a long pole. And on the other side of the ring the human pyramid began to put itself together, with Oliver Winslow at the bottom and Carrington Updike at the top.

Of course Carrington was really cute. He waved his pudgy fists while Weezie clutched his ankles and wrapped her legs around Frieda's neck and Frieda hung on to Rachel, and Rachel sat firmly on Eleanor, and Eleanor clutched Sidney by the ears, and Sidney jiggled left and right on Hugo's shoulders, and Hugo reeled under the weight of the six heavy kids above him, and down at the bottom of the pyramid Oliver Winslow propped up the whole thing, his mighty muscles bulging.

164

Once again there was tumultuous applause, but as soon as Weezie dropped Carrington into Cissie's arms and everybody scrambled down, another act came whirling into the center ring. It was Andy on his unicycle.

He was sensational. His little bike sparkled, his baggy pants were purple and a shaft of sunshine followed him like a spotlight. His unicycle whirled and danced in circles. He was juggling at the same time, gazing up and laughing at his sky-blue balls, tossing them higher and higher, making them fly so high that they merged with the patch of sky overhead and didn't come down.

There were gasps as he twirled his bike around for the last time, jumped down, held up one arm and flung out his hand.

Where had they come from so suddenly, all those elephants? It wasn't just Sita and Rajah anymore; it was a whole parade, elephant after elephant after elephant. Big elephants, middle-sized elephants, baby elephants, they were all marching majestically around the ring, every gray trunk curled around the tail of the elephant in front, except for the trunk of the first elephant, which swayed freely in the air at the very front of the noble cavalcade.

"Come on, please, you guys," cried Andy, springing

165

up on the first gigantic elephant. For a moment the circus performers were flabbergasted, but then they all began scrambling up, the bigger kids helping the smaller ones, until every single elephant in the magnificent procession carried an ecstatic rider.

Eddy sat high on the second elephant, Oliver on the third, Cissie and Carrington on the fourth, Otis on the fifth, Sidney on the sixth, Hugo on the seventh, and Frieda and Rachel on the eighth. The other two elephants were old friends—Rajah was next to last, carrying Eleanor and Weezie, and Sita trudged along at the end of the line with Georgie sitting high on his back, all alone. Rocking easily, Georgie leaned forward and counted. Then she counted again. There were ten elephants in the grand parade, stirring the dust with their forty tramping feet.

Was that all? Only ten? What about the other two elephants? Georgie wanted to call out to Andy and ask him about the eleventh and twelfth elephants, but he was far away at the head of the parade, swaying gracefully from side to side on the back of the first elephant in the procession. Craning her neck, Georgie saw him turn and smile back at her and wave.

It was all right, decided Georgie. Whatever Andy did was surely right.

The audience had already been dazzled, but the

parade of elephants was breathtaking. Everyone fell silent—all the old folks from the nursing home, all the fathers and mothers, grandfathers and grandmothers, all the little sisters and brothers. Everyone watched, awestruck, while the great beasts paced around the ring in ponderous majesty, as though ten great kings and queens had strolled into the circus tent from distant jungle palaces to honor this little New England town.

Around they went, once, twice, three times. And then Andy jumped down from his elephant and ran back to help Georgie slide to the ground from Rajah's lofty back. "It's our turn now," whispered Andy. His eyes were glowing. "Ready, Georgie?"

"You bet," said Georgie.

At the control center, Hugo stared wildly at his list and ran a trembling finger down the order of events. What was next? Was he supposed to be doing something now? At last his finger stopped at the right place. Jerking to attention, Hugo punched a button and the calliope drums began to roll.

Outside the tent Hunky Poole crouched on his knees, staring through the hole he had ripped with his jackknife. His heart was beating fast. What if things happened the way he'd planned? And if they did, *oh, jeez, what would happen then?*

167

44

Elephant Number Eleven

Whenever you hear the roll of drums, you know something big is going to happen.

Aunt Alex sucked in her breath and clutched Uncle Freddy's arm, because Georgie was climbing a ladder. Andy, their houseguest from India, was climbing another. Above them, dangling from soaring cables, trembled a pair of trapezes, like swings on a playground.

But they were not on a playground, they were at the top of this beautiful tent, this fearful and terrible tent. "I should have found out what was going on," moaned Aunt Alex. "I should have stopped her."

"She'll be all right," stammered Uncle Fred. "Look,

there's a net. Even if she falls, the net will catch her."

The drumbeat quickened. Georgie slipped easily from the ladder and sat down on her trapeze. When Andy took his place on the other side, he had his back to her, but he looked over his shoulder and smiled. And then he pointed down.

Obediently Georgie looked down and saw something amazing. Everybody else was amazed too, all the fathers and mothers in the rows of seats, all the babies and toddlers, all the kids from school and the old men and women in wheelchairs.

And then everybody laughed, because one of the elephants was playing hooky. It was sweeping its trunk left and right to pick up popcorn in the center ring, heaving its great body from one fluffy piece to another and curling its trunk to stuff them in its mouth.

Georgie laughed too, but she guessed that Frieda would be really mad.

Frieda wasn't mad; she was afraid. Frieda had not been afraid before, but now all her show-off swaggering fell away. What if Andy was asking too much of Georgie? What if something terrible happened? Frieda pulled off her top hat because it got in the way, and gazed up at the two swinging trapezes. Andy and Georgie were plunging to and fro, in and out, faster and faster.

At this point Frieda was supposed to blow her whistle and shout into her megaphone:

169

LADEEZ AND GENTLEMEN, YOU ARE ABOUT TO WITNESS THE GREATEST AERIAL ACT OF THE CENTURY!

but she couldn't blow her whistle. She couldn't shout.

Only Hugo at the command post didn't see what was happening because he was staring at his list. The next direction was in boldface type:

TURN UP VOLUME!

At once he turned a knob, and the drumbeat rose to an earsplitting thunder.

Then everybody stopped laughing, and Aunt Alex uttered a cry as Andy dropped backward and hung by his knees.

Below them the greedy elephant was still stumbling around gigantically, groping for popcorn. Then to everyone's horror, the stupid elephant blundered against a tent pole, and at once the net collapsed—*because last night Hunky Poole had cut through the knots, leaving only a few threads.*

There were shrieks of dismay. Aunt Alex leaped to her feet, but Uncle Fred reached up a shaking hand and pulled her back down.

Georgie and Andy didn't seem to care. They went

170

right on pumping their legs in and out, faster and faster, swinging back and forth like the pendulums of two clocks.

Georgie began to count, because it was time to fall forward into empty air—*four, three, two*—when another rope parted, and the bar of her trapeze dropped and hung straight down.

For a second Georgie hung on with one hand, but her fingers were slipping and slipping—they were about to let go.

Aunt Alex screamed, Frieda screamed, and Andy screamed in another language. Instantly the careless popcorn-eating elephant rose on its hind legs, lifted its huge head, swept up its great trunk, curled it around Georgie and lowered her safely to the ground.

Aunt Alex fell back in tears. Andy raced down the ladder and took Georgie's hand. Breathing hard, they bowed together and bowed again, while everyone clapped and laughed with relief. *It was only a trick, a clever trick! Bravo!*

In her seat near the entrance to the Big Top, one very important person clapped harder than anyone else. Then Matilda MacIntosh stood up and tripped out of the tent, smiling and nodding to all her best friends.

But everyone else stayed to watch as Andy scrambled up on the elephant's back and pulled Georgie up

171

beside him, and then the heroic elephant carried them grandly twice around the ring while Hugo pushed another button and the calliope went back to "Yankee Doodle" with noisy cymbal clashes and blasts of the mechanical horns.

But when the brave elephant made its way out of the tent at last, Andy and Georgie ducked their heads under the billowing cloth and Georgie grinned, because she understood it now. The popcorn-eating elephant had not been playing hooky after all. It was a new elephant entirely. It was elephant number eleven.

But what about the twelfth? Would there be another elephant, the very last elephant of all?

45

THE HIDEOUS NOISE

*F*RIEDA CLAPPED HER TOP hat back on her head and shouted into her megaphone. It was her last command:

> ***LADEEZ AND GENTLEMEN!***
> ***THIS PERFORMANCE OF THE MISTERIOUS***
> ***CIRCUS IS NOW FINALIZED!***
> ***YOU ARE REQUESTED TO EXIT THE***
> ***PREMISES!***

Well, it was high time. Everyone under the Big Top was worn out by all the thrills and excitement, by one grand performance after another, and finally by the spectacular accident so cleverly staged by the two cute trapeze artists and the funny big elephant. Brilliant! Hilarious!

The elderly folks went first, pushed along in their wheelchairs, and then the families with babies and little kids.

Hugo shut off his electronic equipment and pushed the calliope switch.

At once the noisy music whined down and wheezed to a stop:

YANKEEEEEEEEEEeeeeeeeeeee.......

Shaking with relief, Hugo ducked out of his command post and marched after Frieda, shuffling and hopping to get in step, and then tramping firmly around the ring toward the gap in the tent where Eddy and Oliver were yelling and waving.

Aunt Alex wanted to run after them and find Georgie, but Uncle Fred said, "Wait. She's all right now. She'll be fine."

As for Matilda MacIntosh, she was no longer smiling. Circling the tent, she kept out of the way of the happy band of circus performers and the trampling feet of their idiotic elephants.

Angrily she rounded the far side of the tent, looking for Hunky Poole. Where was that rotten kid? The little brat's mouth would have to be shut up tight or there might be trouble. Police action, lawsuits!

She found Hunky huddling behind a bush, snivelling. "I didn't do it," sobbed Hunky. "I don't know nothing about it."

Matilda hauled him up by the front of his shirt, shook him, and hissed between her teeth, "Listen to me, you little creep—"

But then she stopped and lifted her head and listened, because she could hear a noise.

From the direction of the Mill Brook meadow came grindings and crashings and the sound of roaring engines.

"My theme park!" cried Matilda. "They're here! They've begun!"

46

Noah's Ark to the Rescue

SIDNEY BLOOM AND Otis Fisher were the first of the circus kids to hear the noise from the Mill Brook meadow. They looked at each other in horror, then raced across Walden Street and bounded along a path behind the fire and police station. At the edge of the meadow they took one look at the heavy machinery and came tearing back with the news.

"The bulldozers!" screamed Sidney. "They're here."

"Just listen to that," shouted Otis.

The others listened, and looked at each other with shocked faces. There were groans of dismay.

"We've got to do something," cried Frieda, but for once she didn't know what to yell into her megaphone.

But Andy knew what to do. He threw out a pointing arm and shouted, "To the merry-go-round."

"The merry-go-round?" whimpered Hugo, bewildered. "Jeez, what for?"

But then Frieda's megaphone bellowed the order

COME ON, YOU GUYS, TO THE MERRY-GO-ROUND!

Hugo trailed after the rest of them as they ran after Andy. Frieda led the way. Then came Georgie, Eddy, Sidney, Rachel, Otis, Eleanor, Weezie and Oliver. Cissie Updike was last because Carrington was a dead weight, bobbing up and down under her arm.

At once they were entangled in a happy crowd of wheelchairs and baby strollers, mothers, fathers, sisters, brothers, uncles and aunts, because the entire audience was flooding out of the circus tent and heading for home.

In the confusion Cissie Updike handed Carrington to her mother, who snatched him up, screaming, "Oh, my little darling!" (Mrs. Updike was really weird.)

And then at the merry-go-round there was another problem, because it was occupied territory. A dozen little kids were squealing with joy and rising and falling on the ostrich and hippo, the lion and tiger, the giraffe

177

and gorilla, and once again a couple of teenagers had taken over the dinosaurs. They were horsing around and hollering funny caveman jokes.

Andy jumped up on the moving platform and pressed a button. At once the platform slowed to a stop. Fathers lifted down their moppets, mothers plopped toddlers into buggies and the teenagers loped away, punching each other and laughing.

The merry-go-round was free for the taking. "Come on, please, you guys," shouted Andy, and at once they jumped on the platform and scrambled up on the animals of Noah's Ark, the beautiful painted beasts that were so much like wild forest creatures or monsters from the ancient past.

Once again Eddy found his tiger and Sidney grabbed the lion, Georgie pulled herself up on her brown bear, Eleanor scrambled up on the ostrich and fluffed out her tutu, Cissie settled herself on the moose, Otis straddled the gray wolf and Rachel struggled up on the Brontosaurus. Frieda was small for her age, but somehow she clambered up and sat down again on the tall back of her giraffe.

Hugo was late. By the time he came along, not many animals were left. He failed to find the hippo and he was too timid for Tyrannosaurus rex. Hesitantly he shambled around, looking for his gorilla. At last its fierce

178

glass eyes glared at him and he stopped short and said, "Oh, there you are," and floundered up on its slippery back.

Only the hippo and the Tyrannosaurus were left. Giggling and shrieking, crazy little Weezie Hoskins ran straight for T-rex and tried to swarm up its long lizard tail.

But of course that would never do. Oliver Winslow plucked her off with two fingers, dumped her on the hippo and took over T-rex himself—because who, after all, was the biggest kid with the loudest mouth and the strongest muscles? Who but Oliver Winslow?

47

THE WIMPISH WARRIOR

URING ALL THE WEEKS of getting ready and teaching circus tricks to everybody, Andy had spoken softly. But now he was a gallant knight leading an army into battle.

"Forward!" cried Andy, and at once his mounted warriors felt their animals quiver beneath them. *The painted beasts were coming alive.*

Sidney's lion roared and shook its head, the tiger looked back at Eddy with blazing yellow eyes, Cissie's moose swung its broad antlers, Georgie had to grip the fur of her brown bear as it pawed the floor, Frieda had to throw her arms around the neck of her giraffe, and Eleanor's ostrich pranced, bouncing her up and down.

Rachel's Brontosaurus lifted its lizard head to nibble the striped canopy of the merry-go-round, and she had to kick it with her heels to make it stop. The gray wolf growled and Otis, clinging to its back, was startled to see the fur on its neck rise up. Hugo yelped and wrapped his arms around the hairy shoulders of his gorilla because it was standing on its hind legs and thumping its chest like King Kong in the movies, and Oliver Winslow had all he could do to keep from sliding backward on his dinosaur as it reared and opened its terrible jaw and screamed. And of course Weezie Hoskins, clutching her hippo by the ears, outshrieked even the lion's roar and the screams of Tyranno-saurus rex.

Then, one by one, the animals tumbled off the plat-form. They were a charging army of living beasts. With Eddy's tiger in the lead they hurtled toward the terrible machines that were wrecking the Mill Brook meadow. Noah's Ark was going into battle.

But where was Andy? Clinging to his plunging tiger, Eddy looked back and saw him standing on the platform of the empty merry-go-round, and he shouted, "Andy, aren't you coming?"

But Andy stepped down and turned away, and his shout was too faint to hear.

Eddy's tiger bounded into a thicket, but at the last

181

second he caught a glimpse of gray shapes looming up behind the merry-go-round. *The elephants! They were coming!* And Sidney, lying flat on his striding lion, looked back and saw the churning dust, and Eleanor, jiggling crazily up and down on her racing ostrich, heard the furious trumpeting.

But only Oliver Winslow, bringing up the rear on his towering dinosaur, understood what was really happening. Craning his neck backward and clutching a gristly fold of scales as T-rex threw him up and down, Oliver saw the elephants mill around in confusion. He saw Andy stroll away and disappear in the cloud of dust. Was he deserting them at a time like this? What a wimp!

48

A Throng from Earth and Sky

S THE ANIMAL ARMY plunged past the public garden plots, the cabbages shivered, ripe tomatoes fell from the vines and watermelons wallowed on the ground. The sky was dark with birds, and Hugo, clinging to his gorilla for dear life, blinked as a cloud of butterflies fluttered around his face.

And Georgie, glancing down from the back of her lumbering bear, saw another army on the ground. Thousands of shining beetles were scurrying along beside her. Worms tumbled out of their holes. Snakes slithered in the weedy grass.

And then she laughed, because a rabble army of dogs and cats came streaming out of the houses. There were big dogs and little dogs, yipping and barking, and floods of cats, everybody's cats—swarms of meowing pussycats—Frieda's fluffy tomcat, Rachel's calico cat and the entire menagerie of black-and-white cats from No. 40 Walden Street. Even Aunt Alex's chickens had escaped from their hen yard, and they were all over the place, flapping their wings and cackling.

At Walden Street the animal army did not halt to look for traffic on the road. With Eddy's tiger in the lead—*but where was Andy?*—they poured across to the other side. A flabbergasted driver slammed on his brakes as an escaped zoo of wild beasts streamed head-long in front of his car. At the fire and police station the police chief careened out of his office, sprinted into the road and blew a blast on his whistle, but then he had to skip out of the way of a nightmare from the Maine woods, a moose as big as a truck.

Elephants and chickens, beasts and birds, beetles and snakes, dogs and cats—it was a mixed-up army from jungle and wilderness, forest and field, from chicken house and backyard. It was a throng from earth and sky.

In the Mill Brook meadow the job was well under way. The big machines were hard at work. The air shuddered with the grinding of diesel engines, the shriek of metal

184

on metal and the smash of rock upon rock.

On one side of the meadow a crawler dozer was busily flattening the trees beside the brook, while a big diesel shovel scoured the bed of the stream, lifting muddy bucketfuls into a dump truck. At the edge of the trees a cement mixer stood waiting, its huge barrel turning, making cement for the bottom of the mini–Walden Pond. On the other side of the meadow a tractor rattled and banged, dragging a ripping machine. The ripper clawed at the blossoming field, sinking its teeth into buttercups, and behind it a front-end loader scooped up the clods. Below Heywood Street an excavator opened its jaws and gobbled the remains of an apple tree. There was also a crane as high as a six-story building, its dangling hook swaying, awaiting its turn.

But Matilda MacIntosh could not wait. She scrambled all over the field like a job boss, too excited to watch from the sidelines. But when she stumbled over the rutted ground to inspect the plastic cabin, she was crestfallen. The door lay flat on the ground and the fiberglass dummy was stalled in the doorway. Its mouth was opening and shutting, but there was so much noise from the machinery, Matilda could not hear any of its wise and wonderful words.

The noise was so great and the men at the controls of the diesel shovel and bulldozers and dump trucks were so busy backing and turning their heavy machines and gouging the soil and scooping up bucketfuls of dirt and rock that they failed to see the first battalions of the army of Noah's Ark, the flocks of birds circling over the meadow.

And they paid no attention to the pack of barking dogs and the swarms of yowling cats. But they woke up suddenly when a five-hundred-pound Bengal tiger bounded across the Mill Brook, leaped up on the radiator of one of the bulldozers and gazed through the windshield with its terrible golden eyes.

49

THE BATTLE OF MILL BROOK MEADOW

*T*HE ENTIRE MEADOW WAS in a state of shock. The diesel shovel stopped shoveling, the ripper stopped ripping, the arm of the excavator jerked and hung still, and in a panic the front-end loader dumped its bucket of buttercups on the ground.

Matilda MacIntosh was shaken too. Stumbling around Henry's cabin, she cowered behind its shuddering wall.

Andy and his eleven elephants were still nowhere in sight, but Sidney's lion came streaking across the meadow to attack the outriggers of the sixty-foot crane, trailed by another regiment of squalling cats and barking dogs.

At last the drivers came to their senses and their machines began backing up, wallowing and grinding into reverse, their air horns hooting in alarm, their drivers frantic to get away from this lunatic assault by man-eating beasts, wild jungle animals and—*Holy Moses, what was that? It looked like some kind of—no, no, it couldn't be, but great God almighty, what was it? Here it came!*

It was Rachel Adzarian's Brontosaurus, but soon its massive gallop in the direction of the front-end loader slowed down and stopped. The vast creature lowered its long neck into the Mill Brook and began munching at the weedy bottom of the stream. Rachel kicked at it and yelled, but its dinosaur ears were underwater.

Frieda's giraffe also deserted the attack, stopping in midcanter to reach up and chew a spray of juicy leaves. Frieda was beside herself. She hollered, "Giddy-up," but the giraffe went right on plucking and nibbling.

And then Weezie's hippopotamus decided to take a bath. It plunged into the Mill Brook and rolled and wallowed. Half-drowned, Weezie pounded its thick hide and shouted, "You dumb hippo," but it only sank deeper. She had to jump off and scramble to the shore, while Eleanor's ostrich sprang past her, soaring over the stream in a single stride, and Hugo's gorilla swung across from the branch of a tree. Hugo hung on desperately, his eyes squeezed shut because the whirl of butterflies was still flapping around his face.

Now the rest of the animals of Noah's Ark came bounding across the brook, racing through the trees into the open field and throwing themselves at the metal sides of the machines, attacking the bulldozer, the excavator, the backhoe. Otis Fisher nearly fell off his gray wolf as it plunged at the diesel shovel and sank its teeth in the giant tires, and Oliver's Tyrannosaurus stalked around the meadow on its massive hind legs, opening and closing its reptile jaw and screaming its prehistoric scream.

Even the worms were doing their part. Night crawlers swarmed over the excavator, leaving slimy trails, and a cobra coiled and uncoiled against the windshield of the crawler dozer and lashed at it with its forked tongue, while the man at the controls shrank back in terror.

The birds were attacking too. A flock of Canada geese swooped down from the sky with hoarse cries. Two geese landed on the hood of the dump truck, and stretched their long necks and hissed at the frightened driver.

But now something strange was happening. The machines had stopped backing up. They were no longer in reverse; they were shifting into forward gear. And now they were speeding up, all of them together, rattling forward and roaring. It was a counterattack.

"Weezie," screamed Frieda, sliding off the back of her giraffe, because the crazy kid was scrambling around all over the place, skipping wildly in front of the racing crawler dozer, scuttling under the wobbling bucket of the excavator, jumping carelessly up and down on the clamshell of the giant crane.

Then to Frieda's horror, the clamshell closed around Weezie and lifted her high in the air. There she was, poor Weezie, trapped in a pair of cast-iron claws sixty feet above the ground, swinging in a wild loop as the boom swayed sickeningly left and right.

The animals of Noah's Ark were in trouble too, because the counterattack was making headway. When the excavating machine made a thundering charge at Sidney's lion, it shook its mane and growled and loped out of reach. "No, no," shouted Eddy as his tiger whirled in midair and padded sideways to escape the advancing blade of the bulldozer. Eleanor's ostrich squawked at the snapping teeth of the ripper, then turned and bounced in great strides to the rear, along with Sidney's snarling wolf and Georgie's grumbling bear.

Even Hugo's brave gorilla came to a standstill. Poor Hugo opened his eyes for a ghastly second, then squeezed them shut again, because the butterflies were still dithering around his head. And on the back of his retreating tiger, Eddy stretched his neck, trying to see the traffic on Walden Street. *Where were the elephants? And, good grief, where was Andy?*

50

ELEPHANT NUMBER TWELVE

*B*UT THEN THEY CAME. A shrill swarm of starlings flew ahead of them like an advance guard as the elephants began surging across the Mill Brook with Rajah in the lead.

Water gushed up in billowing fountains as they splashed across. Rachel's Brontosaurus looked up in surprise, the giraffe gaped and stepped daintily backward, and the hippo floundered ashore. Through the woods and out into the open field thundered the elephants, shaking the earth, lifting up their powerful trunks and trumpeting a war cry.

Terrified, Matilda MacIntosh huddled still lower in her hiding place, but all the animals of Noah's Ark bellowed a joyful welcome.

Eleven mighty elephants pounded across the rutted field and charged the counterattacking machines. Sidney's lion roared, Eddy's tiger lashed its tail, and Otis felt the muscles of his gray wolf coil beneath him, ready to spring. Georgie clucked at her bear, Eleanor's high-stepping ostrich bounded after Georgie, Cissie's moose brayed and crashed through a thicket, tossing its antlers, and Oliver whooped as his dinosaur galloped forward on its mighty reptilian legs.

Poor Frieda had abandoned her giraffe, but she shouted orders anyway from the top of a pile of boulders, and Weezie Hoskins, cradled high above the battlefield in the clamshell of the giant crane, stuck out her head and shrieked.

The counterattack by the heavy machines in the Mill Brook meadow stalled at the sight of the herd of rogue elephants. But then a few brave souls shifted gears and stepped on the gas, and soon the others took heart and edged their big rigs forward to face the stampede of elephants and the army of wild beasts from some crazy forest in New Hampshire or some undiscovered jungle in Vermont.

The two sides came together in a violent smash of solid steel and living flesh, of cast-iron buckets and strong gray trunks, of metal teeth and tiger claws. One

193

of the bulldozers rolled over on its side, the cement mixer sank in a hole, and the dump truck careened into the backhoe.

But the iron maw of the excavator yawned and clashed and yawned again, and Sita stumbled and fell to her knees. At once she rose clumsily to her feet, but then another elephant missed its footing and fell heavily to the ground on its side.

It was chaos, a smash-up, a free-for-all. When Eddy's tiger balked and jumped sideways to avoid the clattering tracks of the crawler dozer, he shouted at Sidney Bloom, "Where's Andy—why doesn't he come?"

But Sidney had to handle a crazy tussle of his own, because a couple of chickens were fighting for a foothold in his hair. Awash in feathers, he tumbled off his lion and flailed at the chickens, but they gripped his scalp and gabbled and flapped. "Don't ask me," howled Sidney. "I don't know what the heck's going on."

Then Eddy's tiger reared and plunged as another flock of honking geese flew low and landed all over the field. Eddy craned his neck and stared around at the wreck of the meadow and the foundering elephants and the counterattacking machines. *Would the battle be lost after all? Had Andy really deserted them? Had he sent them into battle and disappeared to let them fight it out by themselves?*

Then everything turned around. Oliver gave a triumphant shout from his high lookout on Tyrannosaurus
rex. "Look," he screamed at Eddy, "here he comes." And
then all of them stared over their shoulders and craned
their necks and saw Andy at last. His gigantic mount
was thundering toward them and shaking the ground.

It was another elephant, the biggest elephant Eddy
had ever seen. It was tall as a church and covered with
shaggy hair, and its curving tusks were fourteen feet
long. Elephant number twelve was a woolly mammoth
from ten thousand years back.

It charged into the Mill Brook meadow and lifted
its strange-looking trunk and bellowed a strange ten-
thousand-year-old scream, shrill and high, and at once
the battle was over. The woolly mammoth and the
eleven other heroic elephants and all the brave animals
of Noah's Ark and all the great flocks of birds and the
armies of worms and snakes and beetles and even all
the neighborhood dogs and cats and chickens—all of
them together had won the day.

Andy hardly needed his last official document. But
when the machines had backed away and all the drivers
and operators had tumbled out and raced to safety on
Lexington Road and Walden Street and Heywood Street,
and after Frieda persuaded the giraffe to reach up its
long neck and rescue Weezie Hoskins from the clamshell

of the giant crane, Andy leaped to the ground from the back of his woolly mammoth and strolled across the battlefield to the place where Matilda MacIntosh stood tottering in the ruins of the plastic cabin. Greeting her politely, he handed her another document.

This one was like a decree from beyond the solar system, a command from the stars in their courses:

BE IT KNOWN:

THAT THE DESTRUCTION OF THE MILL BROOK MEADOW IS TO CEASE AND DESIST, AND THE MEADOW IS TO BE RESTORED TO ITS ORIGINAL BEAUTY AND PERFECTION.

(signed)

Matilda was in a state of shock, but she read the document through, then handed it back with trembling fingers. She did not look at Andy. She ignored the woolly mammoth towering over her and all the rest of the elephants and the entire milling menagerie of Noah's Ark. She was looking fearfully over her shoulder.

"What is that noise?" whimpered Matilda.

Everyone turned to look. On the tipped-over tractor they saw Aunt Alex's bantam rooster. Its tiny chest was thrust out, its head was thrown back and it was crowing lustily:

WHO DID IT? I DID IT! ARK-ARK-AROOOOO!

51

THE BUTTERFLY WIND

*S*O THE MEADOW WAS SAVED.

Of course right now it was horrible to look at. The entire field was littered with broken trees and gouged with ugly holes and wallowing tire tracks, but before long it would once again be a flowering meadow with a brook running through it, a little tree-lined stream dimpling and swirling on its way to the river.

When the tired veterans of the battle of the Mill Brook meadow wandered back to the circus grounds, they found the place teeming with relatives. Some of the mothers and fathers had not heard about the battle, but the rest of them came running. Some of the parents strangled their kids with hugs. The others bawled them out and wept.

Most of the animals were there too. The elephants lumbered all over the field, the giraffe bit off a leafy branch and the ostrich pecked at popcorn on the ground. Rachel's calico cat arched its back at the brown bear, and there might have been trouble, but the bear had its nose in a picnic basket and paid no attention. Sidney's grandmother squealed when the tiger padded by, then laughed as it yawned and sat down to scratch. Hugo's father edged nervously away from the lion, but he laughed too when it stretched out in the middle of everything and took a nap. The moose was no threat either. It put one hoof on a potato-chip bag and licked the salty paper.

Georgie wondered about the worms and snakes, but they had all crawled back in their holes, and the beetles were gone too. Looking up, she saw the last of the geese flap away in the direction of Walden Pond. A cloud of butterflies was still fluttering around, but they weren't bothering anybody but Hugo.

Where were the dinosaurs? Eddy looked for them a little fearfully. After all, the Tyrannosaurus was as tall as a tower and the Brontosaurus was really enormous, so where were they? And what about the woolly mammoth? Had all three of those gigantic prehistoric beasts just disappeared?

Eddy asked Frieda, and she promptly blew her whistle

and shouted, "NOW HEAR THIS! HAS ANYBODY SEEN T-REX? IF SO, PLEASE REPORT TO HEADQUARTERS," but everybody looked blank. Then Sidney turned up his radio and Frieda had to scream to make herself heard. "LISTEN, YOU GUYS, WE'VE GOT TO CLEAN UP ALL THIS STUFF."

Eddy left the clean-up to everybody else because he had something more important to do. He had to find the Brontosaurus and the woolly mammoth and the Tyrannosaurus really fast, because those extinct monsters shouldn't be running around loose—if anything happened, it would be the fault of the Misterious Circus.

Thinking it over, he decided to begin with the public forest on the other side of Walden Street and walk through the woods to Fairyland Pond.

Of course there were no fairies at Fairyland Pond, but there might be two or three prehistoric beasts.

But after thrashing around in the woods for a while and climbing a tree, Eddy didn't see anything but a few branches tossing at the edge of the forest, over there near the highway. By this time he was tired and hungry. It had been a long crazy day. Giving up on the dinosaurs, Eddy wandered back to the circus grounds to tell Andy about the missing monsters.

Eleanor was looking for Andy too. Now that the excitement was over, she felt a little wistful. She didn't find him, but she found Cissie Updike mounting her horse Maizie. Cissie grinned at Eleanor and cantered away, calling, "See you."

Then Rachel appeared with Weezie, who was sobbing, "I don't wanna go home."

"Tell her she's got to," said Rachel, glowering at Weezie.

Eleanor bent down and said, "Okay, Weezie, where do you live anyway? Where's your mother?"

Weezie bawled still louder, and Rachel made a face at Eleanor, reminding her that Weezie's mother was, *you know, pretty hopeless.*

"Oh, right," murmured Eleanor. Then she was horrified to hear herself say, "Well, you can come home with us, I guess, Weezie."

At once Weezie stopped crying, wound her fingers in Eleanor's shirt with a sly smile, and hung on tight. With Weezie dragging behind her, Eleanor walked all the way around the tent, looking for Andy. Instead she found a cluster of parents flattening themselves against the wall because the hippo was trotting by. But then Mrs. Fisher and Mr. and Mrs. Winslow and Mr. and Mrs. Bloom set off to find Otis and Oliver and Sidney and tell them to hurry up because, *honestly,* hadn't they had enough for one day?

And then Eleanor found Uncle Fred and Aunt Alex.

201

They were waiting beside the merry-go-round, which no longer looked very merry because it was dusty and empty and the Brontosaurus had bitten off a chunk of the canopy.

"Oh, hi, there," said Eleanor. She looked around vaguely. "Georgie's around here someplace. And so's Eddy, I guess. Have you seen Andy?"

"No," said Uncle Fred, "but at least we know who he really is."

"Who he is? " Eleanor stared. "Who *Andy* is?"

"He's Amanda," laughed Aunt Alex. "Remember Amanda? Just before we came to the circus, your uncle Krishna just called from India to tell him to come home."

"Amanda!" cried Eleanor. "But he can't be called Amanda!"

"No, of course not," said Uncle Fred. "His name's Ananda. I heard it wrong when Krishna called before. He's a nephew of your uncle Krishna."

"On the other side of the family, of course," explained Aunt Alex. "So he's some kind of cousin, I think." She groped in her pocketbook for Life Savers, because a long gray trunk was swaying in front of her. "I'm sorry it isn't a peanut," said Aunt Alex, offering one on the palm of her hand.

Sita had really come to say a wordless good-bye, but she took the candy politely and moved away to join the solemn parade plodding into the tent. There were only eleven elephants now, of course, but every trunk except the one belonging to the first elephant was wrapped around another elephant's tail.

After the elephants came all the animals of Noah's Ark, except for the dinosaurs, who were still missing. The giraffe had to bend its long neck beneath the filmy curtain and the moose had to turn its antlers sideways, but soon they had all disappeared inside the tent, muttering and purring and softly growling. At once the snowy fabric rustled and folded over on itself, closing behind them.

Weezie Hoskins still had her fist wrapped in the back of Eleanor's shirt. Now she twisted the other in Aunt Alex's sleeve as the entire central organizing committee of the Misterious Circus gathered around Ananda to say good-bye.

He looked a little sad as he held out his hand and said gravely, "So long, you guys. It has been very cool."

Eleanor hated to say good-bye. "Oh, Ananda," she said wistfully, "won't you miss the Misterious Circus?"

"No," said Ananda, "I will not miss it at all," but he was smiling at her very mysteriously.

"Well, what are *we* supposed to do with it?" demanded Frieda gruffly.

Ananda laughed aloud and mounted his unicycle.

"You guys do not have to do anything with it, because I am bringing it with me. When my uncle Krishna sees it, I know he will understand."

From somewhere the calliope was starting up again, clashing and wheezing the only tune it knew, "Yankee Doodle." And then Hugo fought his way out of the folded tent flap, carrying his father's electronic equipment under one arm and shaking his head. "Sorry," he said. "I pushed the wrong button and the dumb music started up again."

Then he had to dodge out of the way of Ananda's unicycle. "Hey," said Hugo in surprise, "what's happening? Where are you going?"

Ananda merely grinned at Hugo, then looked back at the others and waved before disappearing into the glowing hollow of the tent. For the last time the gossamer fabric fluttered and fell, and then the wind began to blow.

The air had been still before the little breeze sprang up. The tent walls had sagged and all the ropes had been hanging slack. But the puff of wind ruffled everyone's hair and then with a sudden *whoosh*, the breeze became a gale that whipped the stakes right out of the ground and whirled the wild ropes in the air and rattled the flapping walls of the tent.

The wind must have started thousands of miles

away and whistled over the Rocky Mountains, picked up speed across the Great Plains, blustered through a gap in the Berkshire Hills and sent a blast of cold air across Massachusetts, blowing away hats, snatching laundry from clotheslines, tossing trees and flinging branches to the ground and ringing the bells in church steeples, before dropping down like a tornado on this small triangle of land in the little town of Concord. Now the wind whistled through the circus tent and lifted it billowing into the air, up and up into the blue sky.

But perhaps there was another reason for the sudden wind. Hugo knew where it came from. "Those butterflies! All flapping their wings at once!"

Sadly the rest of them stood watching as the flimsy tent wallowed in the air, its delicate walls flowing backward like streaming draperies, its pennants fluttering, the banner for THE GREATEST SHOW ON EARTH billowing out like a message for the world below.

Miraculously the calliope was still faintly hooting as the flying tent grew smaller and smaller in the eastern sky, and for a few minutes they could hear the tinny thrumming of the drum.

And then it was gone, everything was gone—tent, banner, music, all the great beasts from Noah's Ark and every one of the eleven great elephants, and with them the great juggler and unicyclist, no longer a problem

205

child but an impresario, a majordomo and the maharajah of a magnificent circus, their cousin Ananda from India.

The sky was empty, except for a few clouds and the scrap of a rainbow.

All that was left on the ground where the beautiful tent had stood were a few pieces of popcorn skittering over the grass.

Uncle Freddy figured it out. The Misterious Circus had been a combination of things. Half of it had been electronic, the work of the boy named Hugo, and the other half had been enchanted, thanks to Krishna's young nephew Ananda.

But hadn't there been another impossible half? Had not the Oversoul been part of it, the mystic substance that was so thick in the air of Concord?

Of course! And therefore, just as usual, Uncle Freddy made a sublime remark. "Let me remind you," he said grandly, "that the greatest show on earth is the earth itself." He pointed up Walden Street. "Just take a look at that tree."

Eleanor pulled herself together and said politely, "What tree, Uncle Freddy?"

"That one over there beside the school. Do you see that tree?"

Well, of course they saw the tree. It was just an

ordinary middle-sized tree, an oak tree or maybe a maple.

"First it was only a seed, but one day it popped up— you know, like your elephants. And then it grew and grew, and just look at it now. Isn't that amazing?"

Obediently everybody stared at the tree and agreed that it was amazing.

Modestly the tree just stood there, a couple of its leaves drifting lazily to the ground.

The leaves had not been blown off by the wind, because it had died down and the air was still. There was another more important reason:

LADEEZ AND GENTLEMEN!
WELCOME TO THE GREATEST SHOW ON EARTH!
THE WONDER OF THE WORLD!
PRESTO, HOCUS-POCUS!
THE CIRCUS TRICK OF NATURE!
SUMMER JUGGLED INTO FALL!

EPILOGUE

*I*n the newspaper next day there was a peculiar story. Fifteen people driving home on Route 2 claimed to have seen monsters crossing the road.

Readers of the newspaper snickered. Those fifteen people had watched too many monster movies. Mass hysteria, that was all it was. Nor did anyone believe the rumor that herds of prehistoric beasts were on the loose in the north woods of Maine.

Dinosaurs, extinct elephants, how ridiculous!

ABOUT HEYWOOD MEADOW AND THE MILL BROOK

The people of Concord have saved them from development before. Both the meadow and the part of the brook that runs through it are now protected by the town of Concord.